MW01717120

Overlooked Legacy of Ted Williams

By

Edward S. Leonard

DEDICATION

This book is dedicated to the memory of Ted Williams, his three business partners and their wives

Notation

This book defines the Overlooked Legacy of Ted Williams from 1957 until 1986

And It Provides

A historical view of the rural town of Lakeville, Mass, during the 1960's

COPYRIGHT

Copyright © 2024

Paperback ISBN: 978-1-964467-75-7
Hardcover ISBN: 978-1-964467-76-4

Copyright No: 1-14758606531

Edward S. Leonard

Overlooked Legacy Of Ted Williams

No part of this publication may be reproduced, distributed, or transmitted in any form or by any means, including photocopying, recording, or other electronic or mechanical methods, without the prior written permission of the publisher, except in the case of brief quotations embodied in critical reviews and certain other noncommercial uses permitted by copyright law.

Table Of Contents

PROLOGUE

THE OVERLOOKED LEGACY OF TED WILLIAMS

The life and times of "The Greatest Hitter Who Ever Lived" - Ted Williams has been documented several times with only a casual reference to an important and meaningful period of his life when Ted gave of himself and his resources for the betterment of young boys and girls. He kept himself out of the limelight while allowing his name to be placed at the head of his effort.

TED WILLIAMS BOYS BASEBALL CAMP

In September of 2023, I received the gift of a book, "The WINGMEN," written by Adam Lazarus and published the same year, stating, "The Unlikely, Unusual, Unbreakable Friendship Between JOHN GLENN and TED WILLIAMS". The book describes the two years Ted gave to his country as a fighter pilot during the Korean War. That became the second legacy of his life. However, it dismisses another chapter in Ted's life with a misleading comment that aroused my attention.

He wrote, "he made occasional cameos at the annual Ted Williams Camp held on 180 rural acres in Lakeville, Massachusetts. Williams regularly put on a show in front of locals and campers aged eight to nineteen by crushing deflated softballs over the fence."

This is a misleading statement! Ted Lived in Lakeville every summer for 8 years. He introduced the game of "Blooper Ball" during a dedication of a town park. It was an oversized softball and a lot softer.

I have lived in the quiet town of Lakeville for 18 years and have driven past the entrance to TED WILLIAMS CAMP hundreds of times without considering its origin. A few years ago, while having a haircut by my barber, Fred Correia, he mentioned that he had cut Ted's hair when he opened his shop in 1960. This was the first year that Ted began living in Lakeville. He told me that Ted noticed a fly casting rod leaning in the corner. Ted's nature was to ask questions, especially of "Regular" people like Fred. He asked Fred if he was a fly fisherman. Fred acknowledged that he was teaching himself to fly cast. Following the haircut Ted gave Fred a fly casting lesson out in the parking lot. This became a long-lasting friendship between the two.

This was the beginning of my delving deeply into the origin of the Ted Williams Boys Baseball Camp. I found that many writers referenced Ted's Camp, but none came close to exploring the depth of Ted's involvement and, thus, the legacy he left behind and one that continues today with the support of the Jimmy Fund.

The definition of a LEGACY;

"The long-lasting impact of particular events, actions, etc. that took place in a person's past."

Ted gave of himself when he, with the help of three "Regular" men from the small town of Lakeville, MA, created a boy's baseball camp. To fully appreciate this phase of his life, it is important to review his total being, beginning with his childhood.

He was born and grew up in San Diego in the 1920s, before the Great Depression, in an impoverished home with little nurturing from his parents.

- San Diego has the mildest weather of any area in the United States, allowing outdoor activity for a child year-round.

- His nature was to be a happy boy full of energy in need of a goal, discipline and someone to show interest in him.

- He found this by devoting his time to swinging a baseball bat and playing ball in a local park that had a director with a professional background in baseball and who provided Ted with the support he needed.

- He also found the support of a couple of neighbors and the family of a good friend. They gave him their personal support by teaching him the sports of fishing and hunting and welcomed him into their homes for family meals.

- He grew tall and thin rapidly, which prevented him from running well and embarrassed him in front of girls. Thus, he became a pitcher and avoided any relationship with girls.

- He was born with exceptional talents, brilliant, excellent memory, a quick learner who was always asking questions to learn more, excellent eyesight, great hand-eye coordination, charisma, honesty, loyalty, and a strong sense of integrity. - He had a booming voice and was always speaking with authority. No bad habits.

- He excelled in typing and developed good penmanship in high school.

- His drive to be the best in what he did was noticed by Major League Baseball scouts who went out of their way to secure him into their ranks at the young age of 19.

- He became "Cocky" because he was recognized by baseball professional scouts to be a great hitter of a baseball, his goal.

- He didn't party, drink alcohol, smoke or date girls. He was strictly into hitting a baseball.

- He studied the best hitters and best pitchers he met in order to reach his goal of being "The greatest hitter who ever lived".

- He found a place where he was welcome as a "Regular" guy while playing professional baseball. It was in a small town in Minnesota. He also learned more about hitting, fishing, and hunting and met his first girlfriend. They all were "Regular" people.

- He added profanity to his vocabulary while fitting in with outdoorsmen. This was his new home while enjoying the new experience of four seasons.

- He became wealthy and a nationally known baseball player while living by his standards of honesty, integrity, compassion, and caring for "Regular" people. - He rejected anyone who violated his person. Unscrupulous writers of the local Boston Newspapers attacked him for his shortcomings, which enraged him. You didn't violate his basic personality. It caused him to react with negative gestures and profane speech, which further aggravated the situation.

- He had compassion for people in hard times and children with illness, offering gifts of money and his personal time to help others while avoiding public notice.

- His career was interrupted by WWII. He enlisted late, further aggravating his relationship with the press. He was called back into military service during the Korean War, which again interrupted his career. But these interruptions never stopped him from working hard to become a better baseball player.

- He was a perfectionist in everything he did.

- He gave up on his first marriage with an alcoholic wife and was unable to offer the nurturing needed by his first child. Two faults that always bothered him.

- He was allowed to give back to others while facing retirement without national attention. He took it! It required his ability, experience, finances, and desire to work with "Regular" people to help young boys and girls become disciplined adults with positive attitudes and gain experience working with others to achieve their goals. Campers who lacked a natural athletic ability could learn to be umpires. Umpires are needed in adult life also.

- He was offered a position by a national firm at a time when it was needed to assist them in marketing their sporting goods with a salary and the time needed to pursue his new legacy.

- He purchased a house in Canada where he could fish in the spring and fall, in the Keys of Florida where he could fish all winter, and a house in the Lakeville area where he could spend the summers helping youth. These were not homes in the general sense when you lived in the same home all year.

- He never owned a home where he could become a nurturing parent. He loved being with "Regular" people.

- He made friends with everyone he met at all levels of society, and they loved him for who he was, especially in Lakeville, MA, where he wove himself into the fabric of this small, quiet town for 29 years, creating a legacy that continues there today, 38 years later.

CHAPTER: 1

TED'S EARLY YEARS 1918 - 1937

Theodore S. Williams was born on August 30, 1918, to May and Sam Williams. May was born in Mexico in 1891. Sam grew up in New York State in 1884 with Welsh and English roots. Sam met May in Hawaii while she was training for the Salvation Army, where he was discharged from the U.S. Army. After moving back to California, she gave up her work to marry Sam in 1910. She suffered 2 miscarriages before Ted was born, and they moved to San Diego. A second son, Danny, was born two years after Ted.

May went back to serving the Salvation Army with obsession, while Sam, with a laid-back personality, opened a small photography shop. May became well known in San Diego for her full-time activity begging money to feed the poor while wearing the uniform of a Salvation Army Soldier She was able to purchase a small house but had trouble paying $20 per month of the $4000 mortgage. John P. Spreckels, a wealthy local philanthropist and owner of a couple of local newspapers, learned of this and quietly paid off her mortgage. He appreciated her efforts to raise money to feed the poor.

May became popular during the 1929 Depression, being observed doing her job with her two sons at her side. Ted and Danny did not enjoy this. It was embarrassing.

When Ted became a popular star playing baseball for the local San Diego Padres, his mother would continue to raise money for the poor by working the baseball stands by telling everyone she was Ted's mother while tapping the tambourine, saying they should empty their pockets for the cause. Ted remembers that he was embarrassed by this and that he didn't have good clothes like his friends in his unkept home. My mother was out in the middle of the street. "Until the day she died, she did that, and It always embarrassed me, and God knows I respected and loved her."

TED COULD LOVE

The Williams marriage drifted apart while ignoring the need to nurture their two sons. The boys went their separate ways. Ted went for baseball, but Danny was always in trouble.

Ted's nature was to be obedient, active, happy, and intelligent. He developed an obsession with hitting something with a baseball bat while a youngster in elementary school. When ten years old, he would see a falling star and say, "Make me the greatest hitter who ever lived."

TED WAS OBSESSED WITH HITTING A BASEBALL

His mother did provide the necessary support for her boys. She sent Ted to a summer camp, but he had to earn his keep by peeling potatoes. She provided him with a baseball glove, a fly casting rod, and a tennis racket to occupy his free time and interests. She did not cook or clean the house. An aunt, her sister, would visit occasionally to help.

When Ted was not playing in the team sport of baseball, a neighbor next door would fill the gap in time to occupy his interests. He introduced Ted to fly casting, which he could do alone in his idle time. This became an important hobby throughout his life. Another neighbor across the street introduced Ted to hunting. A school friend, Les Cassie, had a traditional family life and would bring Ted to his home.

Ted was frequently invited to have a meal with Les and his family, especially on Sundays when a well-planned meal, with all of the extras, was prepared by Les's mother. Ted often wished he had a family like Les. Les's father, Less Sr., would often take Ted on a long Friday night experience to a favorite fishing location. These friends and neighbors provided the nurturing he did not get from his parents. Ted would always say he loved his parents and would provide for them in their senior years, even after they divorced. He did this, including support for his brother and his brother's sons.

TED WAS LOYAL

Ted developed his batting skills with constant practice. During his younger years, he spent many days at a local park with a playground Director of Sports, Rod Luscomb. Rod had a professional background in sports and coaching and cultivated Ted's obsession to learn more about baseball, especially hitting techniques. It is assumed that Les encouraged Ted to hit left-handed while pitching right-handed. You would be a step closer to first base at the end of a hit? Ted was always asking questions. Rod also provided nurturing discipline to a youngster who exhibited a drive in a sport they both enjoyed. "He always wore a grin on his face," Rod said. They became lifelong friends.

TED WAS A HAPPY KID

Ted did very well with his grades in High School. He was intelligent, interested, and quick to learn. The principal awarded Ted and another classmate, upon graduation, an award for excellence in typing. They typed at the rate of 32 words per minute without an error. The first in their class.

His only graduation gift, however, was from his friend Les Cassie Jr.'s father. A fountain pen. Nothing from his parents.

TED WAS INTELLIGENT

In High School, Ted obtained extremely high hitting statistics even while being the team pitcher. He had averages of. 583, 406, and 430 in the years 1935, 1936 and 1937 when he graduated. The pitchers didn't get a lot of batting practice. Yet he practiced on his own while actively playing sandlot baseball at the local park. Always swinging the bat.

Ted grew very tall and slim early, which limited his ability to run. This also became an embarrassment in his personal life at the time. His talent for hitting a baseball made him a leader in a local sandlot baseball competition. He received $5 per game with the "Liquor House" semi-pro team. A teammate, Roy Engle, became another lifelong friend. (Roy later joined the coaching staff at the Ted Williams Boys Baseball Camp in Lakeville, MA in the 1960s).

This experience led to an invitation to join the newly organized San Diego Padres Minor League baseball team in 1935, which paid the 17-year-old $150 per month while still a senior in High School. The Padres joined the Pacific Coast League in 1936 when Ted was 18. Ted was 6'3" tall and weighed 145#. His mother signed off on this as Ted was still underage, and she made them pay her and Sam a bonus of $1000 for their acceptance.

Major League baseball was the only major sport in the nation, growing in popularity. Ted continued to play well while still learning the skill. He constantly asked questions of the best hitters and what they did to do so well?

Bobby Doer, a Padre, and Johnny Pesky were playing members in the West Coast League with whom he developed close relationships. Bobby and Ted became close friends as they traveled together, playing for the same team. They also shared an interest in fishing and hunting, and going to the movies. Girls were not a distraction. They both demanded extra food for their active bodies, trying to gain weight and gain added strength. Ted was charging for meals above the teams' allowance of $2 per day. Management overlooked this because of his demonstrated ability as a hitter.

TED MADE FRIENDS

CHAPTER: 2

TED HIRED BY THE RED SOX 1937 - 1938

The New York Yankees and the Boston Red Sox took note of Ted's hitting talent while visiting San Diego in 1937 to sign Bobby Doer to a contract. Bobby was then playing excellent second base for the San Diego Padres.

"Ted was having the time of his life - I never had so much fun - everything was new - the train rides through Sacramento, Oakland, Frisco, Portland to Seattle, traveling with all the professional players - it was fairyland for a year and a half." Then his worries about having access to his own baseball bats were answered when "He signed a contract with Hillerich & Bradsby manufacturer of Louisville Slugger baseball bats, on April 21, 1937 - In return for a dollar and other considerations and giving them his trademark rights for twenty years he received an unlimited supply of bats paid for by his team." "Jack Hillerich, the CEO, said in 2003 that Williams would be given new golf clubs annually as well as other sweeteners - Whatever he wanted."

Red Sox General Manager Eddie Collins noticed this young hitter during Bobby Doer's game. Collins negotiated with the Padres to sign Bobby to a Red Sox contract. Collins turned his attention to Ted but had to negotiate with Ted's Mother to allow the underage recent high school graduate to sign on with the Red Sox.

The Red Sox finally signed Ted to a two-year contract $3000 for his first year and $4500 for the second year. In December 1938, Ted's mother and father were paid a bonus of $2500, which closed the deal. He went to Sarasota, FL, for training that spring.

The Red Sox hired him even though "he was skinny and awkward as hell." Ted spent the rest of his winter preparing to travel East for Spring Training.

It would be a drastic change for a 19-year-old boy to leave home and his mentors and travel across the country to start a new life. It was difficult to say "Goodbye" to everyone who made this dream to become "THE GREATEST HITTER OF ALL TIME" possible. He was ready with full confidence and a "Cocky" attitude. Bobby Doer, who had become a friend and now a Red Sox seasoned second baseman living in Los Angeles, was asked by Sox Management to escort Ted by train to Sarasota, Florida, for Spring Training. A new chapter in Ted's life was beginning.

TED IS COCKY

CHAPTER: 3

TED BEGINS MAJOR LEAGUE BASEBALL 1938 - 1939

Bobby Doer, a star Red Sox second baseman, escorted his new teammate, 19-year-old Ted Williams, to Sarasota, Florida for 1938 Spring Training. Bobby lived in lived in Los Angeles and was headed there himself. Ted was joining the Red Sox, one of the nation's best American League baseball teams.

The Red Sox was made up of 30 players. Joe Cronin was the Player/Manager and one of the six infield players on the roster, along with Bobby Doer. They had 16 pitchers, three catchers, and five outfielders. Ted was to be a future pitcher but was hired for his demonstrated hitting ability.

The day he arrived at the training facility, he was first greeted by the "clubhouse boy" Johnny Orlando, who exclaimed, "The KID is here." They were expecting Ted, whose reputation preceded his arrival. The name stuck! Bobby then introduced Ted to the Manager, Joe Cronin. Ted responded, "Hiya Sport," in a cocky manner. This youngster immediately took Joe aback with an apparent lack of respect for his new boss.

Within 10 days, Ted had traveled to the playing sites of other Spring Training teams in the league. He did not play well and continued his cocky attitude, which annoyed Joe Cronin. Finally, Cronin had enough of Ted's attitude, and on March 21st he announced that Ted was being sent to Minneapolis.

The assignment was that he was being sent to Minneapolis, Minnesota, to join the Minneapolis "Millers," a Red Sox Triple-A farm team. Cronin obviously determined that Ted needed to mature before he would be ready to play Big League professional baseball. Ted was surprised but took the reassignment with good humor, traveling that spring by train to Minnesota. knowing that he would do well.

Ted's beginning salary of $ 3,000 was sufficient to purchase a new 1938 red Buick convertible, which he immediately enjoyed showing off while driving around the small town of Princeton, 30 miles north of Minneapolis. This is where he was to live and play at the local Nicollet Park field while playing ball with the "Millers." He rented an apartment from a new teammate. The Buick cost $2200.

Ted met the famous Rogers Hornsby, the recently retired 41-year-old greatest hitter of the game. The right-hand hitter was to be a Millers coach. This became the most important help to Ted. It resulted in a remarkable improvement in his hitting ability.

Ted would later say, "Hornsby was the most knowledgeable guy I ever talked hitting with."

He learned from him - "Get a good ball to hit," -"Do not chase pitches," -"Work the count to your advantage," - "Study the Pitcher," -"Know what pitches he can throw,"- "Study-Study-Study." Ted had already begun asking experienced players how they played, but this was an important confirmation of all he wanted to know. This obsession would make him "The best hitter who ever lived." Rogers spent many hours with Ted during the season but was gone at the end of the 1938 season.

Ted still performed immature actions on the field, which drove the 51-year-old manager Donnie Bush to finally say to the Millers owner Mike Kelly, "Either he goes or I go!" Kelly convinced Bush to stay because the Red Sox were committed to developing him as a needed talent for the team to win games. Ted told his manager that he was a hitter and not a pitcher and that he should be placed in the outfield. The pitchers didn't get much batting practice, but the fielders did! Bush placed him in right field, where Ted continued his immature actions. He would slap his thigh and yell "Hiyo Silver" when chasing a fly ball, then turn his back to the action and practice his "swing." He refused to wear sunglasses. He carried on a dialogue with the fans while playing right field. By the end of the season, he had made some progress but still needed to mature.

Princeton became a place where he wanted to live. He was accepted into the everyday life of the locals and became one of them. He stayed in Princeton after the season ended and learned more about fishing and hunting, his second and third loves. He became profane, learning the local colorful speech of outdoorsmen. He didn't smoke or drink. Ted was very intelligent and enjoyed studying all aspects of life around him. He didn't waste time dating girls and was embarrassed to be with them because of his physical appearance. Tall and skinny, 6'3 tall and 145 pounds. He made many close friends in the process. He no longer had to bear the needs and wants of his family in San Diego, which was an embarrassment to him. But he did go home for Christmas.

TED MATURES

CHAPTER: 4

TED JOINS THE MAJOR LEAGUE - BOSTON RED SOX 1939 - 1941

Ted drove his new 1938 Buick Convertable in early 1939 from Princeton, Minnesota, to San Diego, California, instead of using the rail tickets sent to him by the Red Sox for him to report for the 1939 Spring Training in Florida. He wanted to visit home first. When there, he asked Les Cassie, the father of his childhood friend Les Cassie Jr., to accompany him on the drive to Sarasota, Florida. He wanted to share his growth in the Major Leagues with his mentor. Les agreed, and he said he would be proud to do this. They both looked forward to Ted's Spring Training as a Major League Baseball player.

On the drive East, Ted came down with the flu in New Orleans. They arrived three days late for Spring Training. The press anxiously awaited and needed to report on baseball's No 1 Rookie. Everyone had high expectations that this new talent would provide the Red Sox with a good year ahead. Joe Cronin, the Player/Manager, made room for Ted in right field, and with the No. 9 on his back, Ted was now 21 years old, 6'3" tall, and weighing 175 pounds. signed the 1939 players contract for $6500. He focused on becoming "The greatest hitter who ever lived," concentrating on the mental as well as the physical aspects of achieving that goal. The lessons learned from Rogers Hornsby are ingrained into his active mind. He studied all of the good batters and pitchers, remembering each one for their strengths and weaknesses. He practiced using the pitching count to his advantage, waiting for a good pitch before swinging.

Ted had matured, but not enough. He continued to be committed to the thought that runs won ball games and that hitting scores more runs than defensive play. He believed fielding was not as important and continued not concentrating on it.

Ted played the entire1939 season of 154 games against all of the other 15 teams in the American League, ending with a good but not great batting average of .327. It was a distraction getting used to traveling between cities by train and living out of a suitcase with 25 outstanding players who were new to him. Ted aimed to seek information from his coaches, the players, and the "regular" employees he befriended. Johnny Orlando, the Clubhouse Manager who was initially named Ted "THE KID", became one of his lifelong closest friends the year before. Hotel beds were too short for his long body. Games were always played during daylight and often as doubleheaders. (There were no floodlights in baseball stadiums until 1947)

Ted was at his happiest when playing ball. He did not enjoy partying after a game when excited fans and many girls gathered outside the park, looking for excitement. He did not smoke or drink and was still afraid of getting close to girls. He had no experience in his past of dating girls due to his self-conscious thoughts of his ungainly appearance. He would stay in his room practicing swinging a bat and walk later to a theater and to a restaurant for a meal and chat with"regular" people who did not recognize him. Being very intelligent, he would learn a lot from reading, especially from Field and Stream magazine when relaxing in his hotel room. Another activity he spent untold hours doing was tying fishing flies when in his apartment at the Sheraton Hotel in Boston. He also did hundreds of push-ups at a time as a strengthening exercise.

TED WAS A PERFECTIONIST

Ted did his part in helping the Red Sox win second place in the 1939 season, winning 89 games and losing only 62. The NY Yankees took first place with an amazing 106/48 record.

When the season ended, he immediately headed back to Princeton, Minnesota, to mingle with the "regular" people whom he now considered his extended family. They taught him a lot about fishing and hunting in a climate totally different from the mild year-round weather he was used to in San Diego. They also welcomed him back as a friend and not as a celebrity.

Following a day of duck hunting that fall, Ted stopped at a favorite restaurant for a hearty meal and uncharacteristically asked the owner, a friend, if he knew of a "cute girl" he could date. The owner called a girl he knew and asked her to come to the restaurant to meet someone he thought she would enjoy meeting. Doris came down and was introduced to Ted, and they sat and talked. She did not follow baseball and had no idea she was talking with a star player. Nor would she care if she knew. Ted enjoyed her company and started dating Doris Soule, whom he would marry years later.

TED WAS NOW INTERESTED IN ONE GIRL

He returned early to Florida to begin the 1940 Red Sox Spring Training schedule by taking a couple of weeks before fishing in the Florida Keys.

At the beginning of the training season in Sarasota, a prominent Boston sports writer requested an interview with Ted, displaying an attitude toward Ted and his important reputation. Ted sensed this was not a "regular" guy and appeared to have been drinking. Ted brushed him off when he openly wanted to discuss his relationship with Boston fans. Ted turned him down with the abrupt statement, "I do not give interviews to sports writers who have been drinking." This writer never had a good word to say Ted Williams after that.

THE BEGINNING OF TED'S PROBLEM WITH THE BOSTON PRESS

1940 was a good year for Ted. He was now under contract for $12,000, ending the season with a batting average of .344. The Red Sox had a fair year, winning 82 games and losing 72, ending up in 4th place behind the 3rd place Yankees. Ted played in 144 of the scheduled 154 games.

However, this was the first year a few sports writers began to harass him. His popularity, profanity of speech, and a few misplays in the outfield gave them material to sell newspapers to interested fans. Boston had many newspapers competing with each other for increased sales. Some defended him. The Sox defended him to the press. Ted's profanity only got worse. Ted was being his outspoken self, setting the standard that you never questioned his character or integrity.

TED DEFENDS HIS CHARACTER AND INTEGRITY

During the summer/fall of 1940, the United States became heavily involved with supporting Great Britain in the defense of German aggression. The Selective Service and Training Act was created on Sept 16, 1940. All men ages 21-45 were required to register for the Draft. Ted was 22 on August 30, 1940.

Ted registered for the draft on January 23, 1941, while vacationing in Minnesota, answering the question of dependents. He reported that he provided sole support for his mother in San Diego. Initially, the classified him 1A and draftable, but later they reclassified him 3A, which deferred him indefinitely. Controversy over his draft status lasted for months in the press. His hunting was interrupted and his baseball career was in question.

In the spring of 1941, Ted drove from Minnesota to Sarasota, Florida, with his girlfriend Doris Soule. He reported for Spring Training a week late and signed a new contract with the Red Sox for $18,000, an increase of $6000, a substantial salary underwriting his value to the Team.

Upon arrival, a few press reporters criticized him for accepting a postponement because of his statement of sole support for his ailing mother. One newspaper went so far as to send a reporter to San Diego to confirm his statement. This negative publicity drove Ted to further distrust Boston newspaper reporters.

During WWII, many baseball stars and all of the 16 American League Teams continued to play regularly scheduled games. The president and a majority of the nation regarded baseball as essential to maintaining both civilian and military morale at home and abroad. Note: Baseball was the only real national professional sport all through WWII. Basketball, football, and hockey were not established sports leagues in the United States until the 1950's.

During Spring Training in 1941, Ted chipped a bone in his right ankle and did play in the final few practice games of Spring Training. He and Doris drove to Boston, where he received medical treatment. Doris went to live with her brother, who lived in Boston. She obtained a job at the Parker House Hotel.

As a result of the ankle injury, Ted took some weight off his right ankle, which ironically helped with his hitting. He continued to play excellent baseball during the 1941 season. He excelled in his All-Star game play, with everyone congratulating him, including the hated press. One newspaper printed, "The KID has grown up. Ted even softened his reactions from saying, "You can't trust any of those guys," to commenting "I'm willing to call it quit if they are." Ted's mother sent him a telegram after the American League won the game, saying, "Congratulations on being on the All-Star team, Thinking of you, my wonderful son; glad you are getting along so well with the sports writers."

Ted did not party after the game, as it was his habit. He went to his room and wrote a letter to his girlfriend, Doris Soule.

In September 1941, President Roosevelt announced that the United States was prepared to join the Allies following Hitler's invasion of the Soviet Union and the sinking of the German battleship Bismark. The United States began converting manufacturing of peacetime items to products supporting the wartime effort – Cars to Tanks and Baseball Bats to Gun Stocks. Rationing of gasoline and foods also began.

At the same time, a fourteen-year-old boy from Maine hitchhiked to Fenway Park to see Ted Williams play in one of the final games. He arrived one day early and was found sleeping on a park bench by a caring policeman. The officer brought the boy to the police station, where he learned of the boys predicament. The policeman was aware of Ted's interest in kids and called Ted at his nearby hotel. Ted was preparing for bed when he took the call. He immediately went to the police station to meet the youngster and hear his story. Ted brought him to his hotel and had him spend the night in a warm bed. He then brought the excited boy as his guest to Fenway Park to witness warm-ups, meet players, and watch the game. The press learned of the story the next day and gave Ted favorable writings.

TED IS COMPASSIONATE

The year 1941 was going very well for Ted. He was invited to go on national radio for an interview in New York city in September. He arrived at the New York airport with his girl friend Doris by his side and was met by the press anxious to print a new story of the famous Ted Williams. The next day Doris flew back to Boston alone where she was met by anxious Boston reporters questioning her for their story. She told them that they were only "good friends" and that she was not interested in baseball and had only gone to a few games only to watch him play. She added that she enjoyed fishing with him more but not that excited with fishing either. Ted had exposed his personal side to the public and learned not to do it again

TED WITHDRAWS FROM PERSONAL ATTENTION

In the final days of his remarkable 1941 baseball season his batting average dropped from

.406 to .39955 which would have rounded to .400 and thus a record breaking season. The Red Sox management recognized this and suggested that Ted not play the final two scheduled games of the season. Ted response was “A batting record is no good unless it is made playing all of the games in the season." He was determined to playout the season. He was healthy! He took a long walk that night with his friend Johnny Orlando, the Cluhouse Manager, to try to relax.

TED HAS INTEGRITY

The last two games were as a double header in Philadelphia. Ted hit successfully 6 -times in 8 at bats and closed the season with a legitimate .406 record breaking average. It defined his long time goal to be "The Greatest Hitter Who Ever Lived." He didn't stop there. He longed to do better.

TED IS A PERFECTIONIST

Ted returned to Princeton, Minnesota with Doris following his record-breaking year to be with "regular" people and enjoy the simple life with friends and Doris. Then things changed! Ted was out hunting on December 7th when Japan bombed Pearl Harbor. The United States declared war on Japan the next day. Ted was classified 3A rendering him exempt from the draft. Although the classification was a source of contention, the under the new circumstances it could be changed. A week later, the United States declared war on Germany. All things were possible.

Ted said he would "enter the service if called" but was adamant that he wanted to improve his hitting ability and earn more money before that happened. He negotiated a contract in February 1942 for $35,000 an increase of $15,000 over the previous year. "I will enlist at the end of the 1942 baseball season". He began the 1942 season with Spring Training.

During the beginning of the season most of all the Boston baseball fans, their children and even military spectators cheered when Ted came to bat. There were a few 'Boos". There was still a need for a national sports attraction to keep up moral and this was an important factor at this time. The Red Sox was the only distraction in town.

April 1942 news of the war was growing on Ted's mind. He was giving in to the fact that everyone should be supporting the war effort, him included. He was still commited taking care of his ailing mother and concerned that he would be able to support her on a minimal privates salary. Ther was no other family member able to help and the Salvation Army had no provision in their financial structure to assist.

Note: No information was found to explain why his past income would not be available to pay her bills. The war, however, could and did last for many years.)

His marketing manager introduced Ted to a Navy Lieutenant who was recruiting for a new

Navy program to train pilots. The educational requirements for this program had been lowered so that high school graduates could apply. Ted was interested and attended a demonstration at the nearby Squantum Naval Air Station. He attended and was impressed.

Ted confided in his friend Johnny Orlando, who tried to talk him out of leaving another promising year in baseball. Eddie Collins, the Red Sox General Manager, met with Ted and Johnny and offered to pick up the support of Ted's mother if Ted enlisted.

Ted signed the application and took the aptitude exam, which he passed easily. He was sworn into the Navy on May 22, 1942

TED IS PATRIOTIC

CHAPTER: 5

WWII YEARS 1941 - 1945

Doris Soule was contacted on May 23rd, 1942, confirming that she was proud of her boyfriend, Ted Williams. They were not yet engaged. Ted was in the Navy Training Program, which did not allow sailors to marry until they had completed their training.

During his physical exam, Navy Doctors in found in 1941 that he had exceptionally good eyesight. He was able to read from 35 feet away that the average male his age could read at only 25 feet away. "He has an unusually high degree of depth perception," stated the testing doctor.

This helped explain one reason for Ted's uncanny ability to read a pitch sooner than other players, giving him the time to determine whether to swing at the ball or not.

The Navy agreed with Ted to allow him to finish playing out his 1942 Red Sox schedule. During the season, he attended Navy indoctrination courses in math, physics, and navigation at a high school close to Boston.

A few fans continued to harass Ted during a July game in Fenway Park. The "Wolves" caused his latent temper to surface, and he showed it through his actions. One never questioned Ted's character or integrity. He would respond with loud profanity. Joe Cronin, the Red Sox Manager, fined him for his actions with the intent of reminding him not to react like this again. The result made Ted more determined to hit more often and more home runs. "This will show them and shut them up." He finished the 1941 season with his record-breaking batting average of .406.

TED WOULD NOT LET ANYONE QUESTION HIS CHARACTER OR INTEGRITY - EVER

Ted reported entering the Navy Pilot Training Program with many other Cadets, including his friend and teammate Johnny Pesky, at Amherst College on November 16, 1942. Beginning on day one, the program instilled military discipline with the requirement of the Cadets to respect all officers by saying "Sir." This was a new situation for Ted, who was used to doing and saying whatever he wanted to say whenever he wanted to say it. Strangely, it agreed with him without question. The program gave lessons in the sciences of navigation and meteorology, plus swimming and physical exercises.

TED WILLIAMS FENWAY PARK - 1942

(Photo courtesy of Bruce Baptist of Lakeville 2024)

INSCRIPTION READS "Ted Williams poses for fans in 1942. For a full generation, Williams was both the biggest gate attraction and resident batter/artiste (Photograph by Fay Ruby)

NOTE: Above THE WALL appears a Gulf oil sign next to where the current CITGO sign has been since 1965 when CITIES SERVICE was rebranded CITGO THE WALL was renamed THE GREEN MONSTER after it was painted green in 1947.

Lessons in personal attack defense followed by actual flying instructions followed. Johnny Pesky commented how quickly Ted "mastered complex problems within minutes that took the rest of the class an hour." Ted applied himself and excelled in all areas except swimming. As a youngster in San Diego, he avoided the water because he was ashamed of showing off his tall, skinny body. He learned to swim and gave himself a hernia to swim faster than the other cadets. He also accepted the requirement to wear a necktie when formally dressed.

TED ACCEPTED MILITARY DISCIPLINE WITHOUT QUESTION

Ted signed in at the Navel Air Station in Pensacola, Florida, in December 1943 following successful training programs in Acushnet, MA, Chapel Hill, North Carolina, and Bunker Hill Navel Air Station, Indiana. Johnny Pesky did not do as well and was sent to Officer Candidate School (OCS) for training other than that of a pilot. Ted was asked to play baseball at each of the bases because Base Commanders wanted to keep the morale high during the war, and Ted's presence guaranteed this. All the while, Doris, his girlfriend, stayed by his side.

The new assignment was for those qualified for advanced pilot training, with the graduates receiving a Lieutenant's Commission. Ted was commissioned on May 2, 1944, and chose to receive the commission in the Marine Corps Reserves. He trained for combat, and the Marine Corps provided that opportunity.

TED WAS ENTHUSIASTIC, COOPERATIVE, AND DEMONSTRATED GOOD MORAL AND MILITARY CHARACTER

Two days later, Ted and Doris were married with a small wedding party and then left to go fishing in the Florida Everglades for their honeymoon. His decision, not hers! She liked fishing but was deathly afraid of snakes and alligators. She was used to the wild animals of Minnesota - bears and wolves. She saw a snake while walking to a fishing spot selected by Ted. That was it! No fishing there for her. The honeymoon was over.

Ted liked to tell the story of how, on another visit to the Everglades with Doris, he wrestled an alligator, put it in his car, brought it home, and put it in the backyard as a pet. After that, Ted would make up an impromptu story about an alligator to distract a person's attention from a current situation. Imagine him asking Yogi Berra if he had heard about an alligator that had been found in the Yankee dugout the morning of a major league game.

TED HAD A SENSE OF HUMOR

His hopes for orders to be sent to the Pacific for combat were dashed because the war was nearing the end that summer - 1944. He was assigned to be an instructor of new pilots and was to remain in Pensacola. The Base Commander wanted Ted to play for the Base baseball team. He lost his enthusiasm for both the military and amateur baseball.

When he had time off, he took Doris fishing in southern Florida. The Keys became his favorite fishing location for winter relaxation. Doris was having trouble accepting all of Ted's demands and their feisty relationship was suffering in private.

Then, he received orders on August 3, 1945 to report to San Francisco for deployment to the Pacific. He was given a furlow for a month and again went with Doris to Florida for more fishing.

Three days later on August 6th, the U.S. dropped the Atomic bomb on Hiroshima, Japan, and a second one on Nagasaki on Sept 2nd. when Ted was in San Francisco. Orders were to be followed with Ted arriving in Hawaii by Ship on Sept 4th.

The War was over, but Ted had to wait 4 months before he was sent back home. The Hawaii Base Commander put Ted on the base baseball team. Ted wanted none of it, and it showed in his performance. He was put on an old battleship in Pearl Harbor with sixteen other servicemen, arriving in San Diego on December 4th, 1945.

His ailing mother, Mary and wife, Doris, met him on the dock. They spent the next few months together, catching up for lost time, reacquainting themselves with the old neighbors, and adjusting to normal life. He was placed on Marine Reserve Status and released from active duty, on January 12, 1946.

Red Sox Manager Joe Cronin flew out to San Diego to sign Ted to a new 1946 contract for $40,000, an increase of $10,000 from his last 1942 contract. He bought a brand new Cadillac convertible, which he and Doris drove back to Sarasota, Florida, for Spring Training. They traveled with and old friend, Earle Buckner and his wife, also from San Diego, who was now a coach with the Philadelphia Athletics. Ted couldn't get there fast enough. He wanted a couple of weeks of fishing before the start of the 1946 season.

TED COMPLETED THREE YEARS OF MILITARY TRAINING – 1946

CHAPTER:6

MAJOR LEAGUE AGAIN 1946 - 1952

Ted, with his wife Doris, arrived at Payne Park in Sarasota on February 25th, 1946 for the first day of Spring Training. Ted kissed her goodbye, and she was off, driving to Boston with the goal of finding and renting a suitable apartment. Major League baseball got off to a booming start following WW II.

Many professional ball players, including stars like Ted Williams and his old teammates Johnny Pesky, Bobby Doerr, and Dom DiMaggio, and clubhouse manager Johnny Orlando returned, ready to resume their careers. The fans were ready also. The sixteen American League teams recorded a record attendance of 20,000,000 for the year. Many needed to regain their physical playing condition. Ted now weighed 195# and targeted 185# when the regular season began.

Even though Ted's legacy was established before his return from the war, he was determined to exceed his prior accomplishments and said so. He was also ready to defend himself against any rude comments that might later be written of him by over-Zelos sports writers. "Colonel" Dave Egan, the upstart Boston sports writer, showed up again, degrading Ted's character. Ted could not lose his dislike for these attacks- ever.

Ted's fame attracted sponsors that required him to hire a new business manager Fred Corcoran, brother of his friend John Corcoran a local Ford Dealer. Wilson Sporting Goods was one of the first sponsors of the new Ted Williams Enterprises. The contract was confirmed with a handshake. Ted trusted regular people.

Early in the season, Ted was hitting above his .406 high and going strong into the mid-season All-Star Game. It dropped afterward, to .360 in September the Cleveland Indians player-manager created the "Boudreau Switch' by placing all his fielders to the right of second base. It got to Ted's head, dropping his season average to .330. He still continued his obsession to hit the right field until he finally agreed that the "Switch," which was being tried by other teams, was affecting his concentration. He decided he would work harder to learn to hit both fields.

September 13 proved to be the answer to his promise to hit the left field on purpose. At the same time, he hit his only career inside-the-park home run against the crafty Cleveland Indians "Boudreau Switch" with a lofted ball over the head of the left fielder who was playing close to the infield. The ball rolled and rolled to the left field wall with the fielder chasing it. Lanky Ted ran as fast as he could and made it home safely.

They won the American League pennant in 1946. 105 wins - 50 losses crafty "Colonel", now a Boston Globe columnist, made up a story that Ted Williams was "Up for Sale" with no basis in fact. It again bothered Ted. R1 pg 269

Ted injured his right elbow in a warm-up exhibition game before the series began when he was hit by a pitch that didn't curve as expected. It prevented him from hitting well in the World Series, which the Red Sox lost to the Saint Louis Cardinals 3-4. This turned out to be what he considered to be the worst failure of his career. Ted's despair for hitting only .200 in the 1946 World Series. In reality, it was not a failure, only a situation that made it seem so. He never complained that his sore elbow prevented him from doing well during the World Series.

"Well, it was over, and I was just so disgusted and unhappy that I couldn't believe we'd lost. I was shell-shocked. I was so disappointed in myself. Just sick inside. I gave my series check to Johnny Orlando, the clubhouse boy who had always consoled me when I was down.

I remember I went over to the train that night. I had been reading these stories about being traded, and now we'd lost and I went into my little compartment on the train. And I didn't come out until about ten thirty. When I got in there and closed the door, I just broke down and started crying. I looked up, and there was a whole crowd of people watching through the window."

TED HAS HUMILITY

Ted continued his obsession to be "the best hitter who ever lived."

Ted and Doris went fishing in Florida for the fall and winter, returning to Boston in February 1947 to sign a contract for $65,000 plus an attendance bonus, which would bring his total income for the year to $75,000.

Ted wore a necktie to the Writers Dinner that fall, where he was awarded the team's MVP for 1946. He did so at the recommendation of his new business manager, Fred Corcoran.

Ted reported for spring training with a positive attitude that he would do well, driven by his poor 1946 performance. The Brooklyn Dodgers accepted Jackie Robinson as the first Black player into the Major Leagues. Ted sent him a letter of congratulations. Ted was being himself. He played against blacks in high school and in the Pacific Coast League. Black people were his equal.

TED DID NOT DISCRIMINATE

1947 was an average year. Night Baseball became a reality with lights added to Fenway Park. Baseball had been softened beginning in 1943, and long ball hitters like Ted could not hit as many home runs. Ted changed his approach by hitting left field and making more base hits. The American League won the All-Star Game with Ted hitting well. Ted ended with a.343 batting average ahead of Joe DiMaggio of the Yankees but lost the MVP to him by one vote. The Yankees won the World Series.

Ted and Doris rented a five-room apartment for a short time in a three-decker in Brighton in the same building with a teammate and his wife. It was here that they announced to the public that Doris was pregnant. They made an arrangement for her to stay in Boston after they returned from Princeton, Minnesota, in the fall and the holidays, where Ted could relax with old friends for fishing and hunting, and Doris could enjoy visiting with her parents over the holidays. Doris was pregnant and expecting on February 15th, 1948.

"The Red Sox erected lights, and night baseball came to Fenway in 1947."

Ted renewed his 1947 Red Sox contract by mail from Princeton, MN, on January 6, 1948, forgoing the traditional signing ritual and party in Boston. He sent Doris to Boston to stay with friends while he drove to the Florida Everglades to do some serious fishing.

He planned to return to Boston the first week of February to be with Doris when their child was born. Nature had other plans as Doris delivered their daughter "Barbara Joyce" three weeks early on January 28th. It took a couple of days to locate Ted in the Everglades and a couple more days for him to return to Boston and be with his wife and Daughter, now called "Bobby-Jo." A boy was hoped for.

The press again went hard on Ted for being away fishing when the baby was born. Ted's reaction was as expected. "Damn the press. It's none of their business." He moved the family into a larger rented home in Newton and provided Doris with nursing care. And with the new entertainment called Television. Ted returned to Florida to fish before spring training began shortly afterward.

1948 Spring training began with little fanfare. The Red Sox started the season poorly, but Ted played well, with a .374 average at the end of May. The Red Sox gained first place by the end of August. The Boston Braves improved during the war years and won the National League Pennant. Maybe a World Series would be between the two Boston teams? It didn't happen. The Cleveland Indians won the American League Pennant and the World Series against the Braves. Very disappointed, Ted ended the season with a great average of .369 and the batting title.

Dr Sydney Faber of the Boston Children's Hospital began a Fundraiser in 1948 with a radio interview of a 13-year-old boy with cancer. All children died of cancer up until this time, and he was gaining success in treatments with chemotherapy. The Fund Raiser was renamed the "Jimmy Fund," with the real name of the child withheld. The Boston Braves and their well-known players adopted the Jimmy Fund as their charity. The players would make visits to sick children. Their work spread throughout the country. Ted Williams met with Dr Faber and began his own private visitation activity.

The Boston Braves left Boston in 1953, and the Red Sox assumed the Jimmy Fund as their charity, with Ted assuming the position as their sponsor, attending many fundraising events by local organizations everywhere as time allowed. He, however, demanded that his many private visitations remain out of the public eye. No newspaper articles. His name continues to be used to support fundraisers today.

TED WAS COMPASSIONATE

Ted was playing to end the 1949 season with another .400 average. That didn't happen. He ended with an average of .342 but was awarded the American League Most Valuable Player. The Yankees won the pennant one game ahead of the Red Sox, who had 96 wins and 48 losses (144 games total)

Ted and Doris, with baby Bobby-Jo, retired again to Princeton, MN, where Ted again fished, hunted, and relaxed with old friends and Doris with family and friends, showing off the baby.

After the holidays, they retired to Florida's warmer climate. Doris went by train, and Ted drove his brand-new powder blue Cadillac. They rented a cabin in the Everglades for a month or more fishing before the start of the 1949 season. His new contract was for a base salary of $90,000, up by $15,000 from the previous year. "The highest-paid player in the history of the game." He also benefited from a bonus if attendance at Fenway Park exceeded 1.6 million. (1949 attendance was 1,596,650) His obsession continued to be "the most successful hitter in baseball" and was achieved again.

Before Spring training began, he experimented with fishing in the Florida Keys. It was such a good experience that he decided to buy a house there and return every winter. Ted and Doris, with Bobby-Jo, rented a very nice furnished apartment in Sarasota before he reported to 1949 Spring Training. Old friend and clubhouse manager Johnny Orlando was ready for him. Ted even got to pilot a DC-4 Red Sox charter flight returning from a practice game in Miami. He is very happy.

The years 1949,1950 and 1951 were nothing special, and he followed his routine in the off months. He recovered from a broken arm in 1950 and signed endorsements with Quaker Oats Root Beer and Chesterfield Cigarettes (He didn't smoke and regretted this endorsement). He also was paid $10,000 for appearing at the fall Boston Sportsman Show, demonstrating fly and reel casting fishing techniques.

Ted was promoted to Marine Corps Captain while serving in the Reserves on Jan 1, 1951. Then, on January 9th, 1952, his life was about to change again. While fishing in the Keys, he received a call from his agent Fred Corcoran, who said that he was being recalled to active service by the Marines to be a fighter pilot in the Korean War.

CHAPTER 7

KOREAN WAR 1952 - 1953

Ted was not prepared for the news of being recalled to active service on January 9, 1952. He was upset but accepted the assignment to appear for a physical on April 2nd. He appeared for Spring Training on March 1. The newspapers and fan base were also upset that their hero would no longer be available for their entertainment. Ted thought that it might be the end of his baseball career.

The Red Sox celebrated a "Ted Williams Day" at Fenway Park on April 30 when he was presented a gift of a new Cadillac by friends and a "Memory Book," with the signatures of 430,000 fans wishing him well for the future. The Red Sox said they would pay him his full $85,000 1952 salary while he was gone to the Korean War. Ted thanked the fans and Red Sox "from the bottom of my heart," waving his hat.

Ted hit a winning home run against the Detroit Tigers on April 30, 1952. The crowd went wild. His sports writer nemesis Dave Egan wrote that morning that Ted was not a role model to kids. Ted, for once, ignored this attack by a writer who should have been fired.

In Ted's fashion, he threw a party that evening, hosting only the many middle-class people, mostly young people, who he considered his closest friends. No ball players or "Big Shots" were invited. "The core group was the so-called Thirteen-Year-Olds, a reference to eight Bostonians who had been close to Ted for the thirteen years he had been with the Red Sox since his rookie year of 1939. His old pal Bill Greeley who managed Jimmy O'Keefe's saloon where the party was held, was there as theatre manager John Buckley, State Cop John Blake from Foxboro, former Red Sox batboy Freddy Stack who was now a fireman, Ted's dentist Dr. Sidney Isherwood, former Sheraton Hotel bellhops Dave and Chick Hunter, and Johnny Benedetti who had lived in the suite next to William's in the old Canterbury Hotel. Also attending were Ted's manager, Fred Corcoran, and Dr. Russell Sullivan, his medical confidant on the Korean call-up. Ted also allowed George Carens, a trusted Boston Traveler newspaper writer, to attend and to chronicle the evening."

He passed the physical and reported for active duty on May 2nd, 1952, thinking it wasn't fair. The Korean War started in 1950 with Marine pilots, both Active and Reservists, having been called to service. The war continued longer than expected, and more Marine pilots were needed.

Ted's marriage was faltering, and his departure for an indefinite time was not going to help. Doris, Bobby-Jo, their daughter, who was 4 years old, did arrive with Ted and stayed at the Willow Grove Navel Air Station outside of Philadelphia, PA. Ted continued on and was greeted with some fanfare from sports writers and base personnel. Flight began immediately with combat training in the classroom and in the air, but not in a jet plane yet.

He was soon transferred to Cherry Point, N.C, the largest Marine air base in the U.S., where he began learning to fly the faster, more maneuverable jet aircraft. Doris, Bobby-Jo, and Ted stayed at a house off-base that was pre-arranged by a local friend of Ted's

Ted immediately applied himself to update his knowledge of flying in combat. He had a natural talent and enjoyed a new, disciplined career piloting the faster, more manoeuvrable jet aircraft. He received a personal commendation after a few weeks in training from the Marine Corps General Commandant, recognizing that he accepted his reassignment to active duty without complaint and he demonstrated exceptional abilities as a Marine Fighter Pilot.

Ted rejected the post Commanders request that Ted join their Cherry Point baseball team. This reactivated his distrust of the reason for his recall.

Ted was attracted by another woman, Evelyn Turner, during this period. A character flaw was now evident. This interlude was interrupted when, on November 14th, 1952, he was instructed he would be leaving Cherry Point On December 8th and granted a leave until the end of the year. On November 16, 1952, he received word that his father had died while in a senior living home in Oakland, CA. He left to attend the funeral, which rekindled his love yet detachment from his family. He was only 33 years old, and his testosterone was at a high level. Difficult and confusing days for Ted. He arrived in California on Jan 2, 1953, en route to Korea.

He arrived at Air Base K3 in South Korea and was assigned to primitive quarters in a Quonset hut with other pilots. Their toilet was an outhouse. He flew his first of many combat missions on Feb 16, 1953, as the "Wingman" for Major Marvin "Pinky" Hollenbeck. They met to review their objective with special instructions for Ted not to endanger himself on this event. The jet plane was equipped with three bombs, and rockets to be dropped, and cannons for protection. Ted lost contact with the Major during a low-level bombing run and was hit with ground fire that severed his hydraulic system. His radio also malfunctioned. A young marine pilot of the mission noticed that Ted's plane had oil running down the side of the fuselage and when he pulled alongside Ted's plane, he had to use hand signals to have Ted follow him back to safety.

The 125-mile flight south to the 38th parallel was full of adventure, climbing to a high altitude and running low on fuel for the glide home. Ted had to land his plane on a strange airbase without landing gear, at high speed and flamming. He slides on the ground for a mile before coming to a halt. The flame was out, but he had to burst the canopy open full himself out, and run like hell away from the wreck. Ted only suffered a sprained ankle due to the pressure he put on it trying to apply a brake system that didn't work. Three days later, he was back flying the remainder of the 39 total missions he flew during the war. In his spare time, he went fishing.

This event became a major news story back home, and Doris was notified. Ted notified his girlfriend, Evelyn Turner, by letter. The sports world was shaken.

Back at the K3 airfield in South Korea, Major John Glenn had arrived from the States to become a combat leader. They were to live together in the same Quonset Hut Officers' quarters. Glenn and Ted became friends, and John learned of Ted's abilities and selected him to be his Wingman. He was aware of Ted's baseball fame but it never became a topic during their working closely together.

Ted suffered from continuous chronic bronchial problems, interrupting some of his combat routines and affecting his hearing, which continued the rest of his life. He, however, received many medals for his service.

When Ted arrived back from Korea, he found Doris to be a confirmed alcoholic. Ted and Doris had many arguments over the years, and Doris enjoyed drinking. Ted's travels while playing baseball, serving in the Marines during WWII, and away from home while he served in the Korean War had taken its toll on their marriage. Ted responded by ignoring the problem that grew over their nine years of marriage. The press was unaware of the growing problems. Ted separated himself from their marriage at that time.

Ted was formally discharged from the Marines on July 28th, 1953, in Washington, DC. He promptly drove to Boston to resume his baseball career with the Red Sox. He went directly to Tom Yawkeys office unannounced, saying, "I'm back!" The surprised Yawkey convinced Ted to go down to the field and hit a few during the practice session for the upcoming game against the Chicago White Sox. A surprise to everyone there.

'He must have hit about twelve out of the park," said practice pitcher Paul Schreiber during the warm-up session. "It was the greatest display I ever saw."

THE KID WAS BACK!

CHAPTER 8

MAJOR LEAGUE AGAIN 1953 - 1957

Active with the Red Sox beginning at the end of July 1953, Ted applied himself with a full practice routine structured for his needs.

At this time, he signed a new contract for an unknown amount of money to complete the 1953 season. (A percentage of his prior 1952 contract of $100,000) He also signed this time the contract for the 1954 season for $100,000)

He had bleeding hands from the many hard-hitting sessions for the next two weeks. His hands are calloused while wearing golf gloves. He then started pinch-hitting during scheduled games. He hit his first home run in the second game he played. The 27,000 fans gave him an extended applause, and the dugout exploded.

Ted was back in the full lineup on August 16 and completed the year with one of his best performances, while the Red Sox had only an average year.

The Red Sox had just assumed the Jimmy Fund as their charity from the departed Boston Braves. Ted was already making unknown visits to children with cancer and other health issues. The Red Sox wanted to do something to welcome Ted back into their schedule but were put off by Ted until someone suggested a Jimmy Fund dinner for donors at $100 per plate. Ted readily accepted this option to support the Jimmy Fund. One thousand people, including celebrities, proceeded to the Boston Hotel Statlerin in an automobile motorcade, Ted riding in one of them.

The fund received $150,000 from this dinner. Ted started off wearing a neck-tie but removed it during the party. Ted did not wear neck-ties except as a required discipline while in the Marines.

Ted returned in the fall of 1953 to his new home in Islamorada in the Florida Keys to do some serious fishing. Doris stayed in their other home in Miami with their five-year-old daughter, which began their separation.

On January 19, 1954, Doris filed for a divorce on the grounds that Ted had been physically and mentally abusive. Ted was known to be profane, and when upset with something, his vocabulary could become obscene. Ted knew that their marriage was in trouble but chose to ignore it. He continued to devote his time to playing baseball, fishing, and exploring other distractions, including women, especially Evelyn Turner. When the press learned of his failed marriage, they explored and publicized his relationship with Evelyn, who responded that she and Ted had been friends for many years, acknowledging she knew he was married.

The subject of physical abuse was a debated issue with some basis of truth stated by their daughter Bobby-Jo in later years. Her brother made known that Doris had her own problems that were aggravated by their life styles and personalities.

Doris asked for their Miami house, their Cadillac, custody of their daughter and sufficient money to live their lifestyle. Ted granted it. He felt some remorse, especially after having failed as a father to his daughter, just as he experienced in his youth.

Her health got steadily worse, living as an alcoholic, another failed marriage, and then alone again developing Alzheimer's.

While fishing at his home in Islamorada in the fall of 1953, Ted met Louise Kaufmann, the wife of a wealthy Ohio businessman and mother of five children. They owned vacation property on the Key Island. She was an excellent fisherwoman in the sport fishing community. Her marriage was in trouble. She spent most of her time in Islamorada with her husband, who was working in Ohio. This is where and when Ted met Louise. Their relationship became close with other neighbors relaxing in the mild climate of southern Florida.

On March 1, 1954, Ted broke his collarbone in spring training. He went to Boston to have it operated on, which resulted in his thinking about retiring. He even announced that this would be his final season. He recovered physically and became more involved with coaching and hitting with his teammates. The Red Sox did not do well over the next few years. Ted stayed on. He continued with his desire to hit well and did. His batting averages were .345 / 1954 ; .356 / 1955 ; .345 / 1956 ; .388 / 1957 earning $100,000 each year. He was drawing cards, filling the seats at Fenway Park.

Ted enjoyed close relationships with three women before and after his divorce from Doris became final in 1955. His second relationship was with Nancy Barnard, whom he met during spring training in 1956. This went nowhere.

Then, he met Isabel Gilmore during spring training in 1957. She was divorced with two sons. Ted courted her and spent time with her sons, who accepted him. She loved Ted but expected more than Ted could give. No profanity and living a normal family lifestyle. Ted even had the boys attend Ted's baseball Camp in Lakeville with lavish gifts and perks. It didn't work. The boys asked to leave after a few weeks. She still loved him and visited him when he was dying 45 years later.

Ted appeared annually at the Boston Sportsmans Show, demonstrating his fly and reel casting abilities. They paid him $10,000 for a week's appearance. In 1957, a member of a long-standing Miramachi Anglers Association invited Ted to be his guest at their Lodge in Gray Rapids, New Brunswick, Canada, on the Miramichi River, which provided spectacular salmon fishing. Ted accepted. He went there that fall and fell in love with the whole experience. The people there were committed fishermen. They were "regular" people. The required guides were also regular guys who accepted Ted not as a famous ball player but as a serious fisherman who spoke their language speckled with profanity.

Ted was busy in 1957, but something was missing in his life, such as a wife or a vision of his pending future without baseball. He felt his growing age and would be retiring from the Red Sox in three years.

Then something happened. A stranger named Albert Cassidy appeared at Fenway Park later in the season, standing behind the railing between the dugout and batting cage before a game. Albert called to him, and Ted responded. The 40-year-old Cassidy had prepared a proposal for purchasing an existing Boy Scout Camp in Lakeville, MA, 30 miles south of Boston, which would make an excellent Boys Baseball Camp. Ted showed interest but had to finish up the 1957 season and needed to get back to work warming up for the game, saying, "I'm interested. I'll get back to you."

THE "OVERLOOKED LEGACY OF TED WILLIAMS" BEGINS

MIDLOGUE

Ted Williams now needs a life-changing activity where he can use his talents and resources to add a meaningful experience to his life. He is nearing the end of his baseball career and has gained the comfort that he served his country in a time of need. The previous chapters document the development of his character and mentality. He was born to be happy, considerate, determined, and loving. He was brilliant, had a great memory, and was gifted with extraordinary eyesight. He learned that he was missing the life of a close family relationship and having a stable home relationship.

He became boisterous, demanding, and frustrated yet successful in his drive to be "the greatest hitter who ever lived." Because of his ability to hit a baseball long and frequently, he became the highest-paid ball player. He drew the largest attendance of fans for the Red Sox, the team he played for during his 21-year career.

He outgrew his gangly appearance to become handsome. He overcame his avoidance of women to the extreme. They loved him, and he loved them.

The disappointment of not developing close ties with three children and three wives was lifelong. His profanity, temper, and the demand for perfection of himself and those he loved that he knew were the reasons for his frustration.

Ted was ready and in need of a project that would allow him to be who he wanted to be with "regular" people. He had the latent desire to give of himself and his resources to help others develop integrity and character in their lives. The focus on youngsters as "regular" people in a fun environment would be desirable.

The opportunity presented itself with the enthusiastic vision of a "regular" guy who interrupted Ted's batting practice one day at Fenway Park in 1957.

THUS BEGINS THE "OVERLOOKED LEGACY OF TED WILLIAMS"

CHAPTER:9

OVERLOOKED LEGACY BEGINS 1957 - 1958

The Red Sox baseball season ended on June 29, 1957, at Yankee Stadium with a 3-2 Win and a season Won-Loss record of 82-72 (154 games played). Ted had a good season with a .388 batting average and a well-earned season salary of $ 100,000.

It was about October 1st that Ted drove 40 miles southeast from Boston over two-lane roads in his new $5300 Cadillac Convertable to meet Albert H. Cassidy in the town of Lakeville. This would be the second time they would meet. This time, they visited the Boy Scout Camp property that Al was proposing they purchase to create a Boys Baseball Camp.

Ted must have been very positive that day following a great season. He had just visited the Miramichi Anglers Association as a guest at their Lodge in New Brunswick, Canada. He loved it! Ted had decided to build his own fishing lodge there in the near future. He had been divorced since 1955, and his 7-year-old daughter Bobby-Jo was living comfortably with his x-wife Doris in the house they owned in Miami, FL. Ted was to sign a new 1958 contract with the Red Sox for a record $125,000.

It was a mild sunny day driving to Lakeville with the top down. In 1957, Lakeville was a small, sleepy town with a population of 3000. It was spread out over three separate villages, each with its own elementary school. High school students went to the adjacent city of Middleboro. The town did not have a shopping center, sidewalks, a traffic light, or street lights. Four narrow roads connected Lakeville to Taunton, Middleboro, Fall River, and New Bedford. They were named TAUNTON ST, BEDFORD ST, RHODE ISLAND RD, and MAIN ST, which connected it to Main St in Middleboro. PRECINCT ST is another country road that connects MAIN ST to RHODE ISLAND ROAD, where the Boy Scout Camp entrance is close to the town center.

The entrance to the 160-acre Boy Scout Camp is from PRECINCT ST through a wooded forest that opens up into a large grassy area with two baseball fields and room for the many pup tents used by the Boy Scouts. It also has its own Loon Pond, which is used by scouts for swimming, boating, and fishing. Many small buildings were scattered close to the pond and used for housing staff and storing equipment and crafts. There is an Office building, a large dining hall, and tennis courts.

Lakeville is a rural community with many farms. The town center had an old Town Hall building and Library facing Bedford ST. There was a Convenience Store named "MY WIFE and I" on BEDFORD ST. Across the street is Assawampset Pond, Massachusetts's largest natural freshwater body.

"MY WIFE AND I - The Booklet - "LAKEVILLE Then and Now “a pictorial history” dated August 1993

Printed the following photo and description of "My Wife and I" convenience store.

"FROM 'MY WIFE AND I TO BIRCHWOOD COMMON"

"For several decades in recent history, a convenience store on Bedford Street, with an interesting name and a fine lake view, served food, sold newspapers, liquor, groceries (and sometimes shoes) and pumped gas to thousands of Lakeville customers.

It acquired a reputation as the favorite coffee-and-doughnut hang-out for those seeking to exchange or collect town news.

During its golden years, "My Wife and I" became popular enough to be the subject of a picture postcard.

Eventually, environmentalism caught up: the location of the gas pumps contributed to the store's demise. In 1985, a shopping complex named Birchwood Common was built at the rear of the property, previously the location of Linden Lodge.

Linden Lodge located behind "My Wife and I" store before it was demolished in 1977 photo courtesy of the Lakeville Assessor's office

Note: Ted Williams may have stayed overnight here—a few nights in October 1957, when he made his first visit to meet Albert H. Cassidy and Bernie Cassidy. Then, he met with Lester Warburton.

The convenience store had a "Do It Yourself" gasoline pump outside and a general grocery store inside with a "Soda Fountain" bar that served ice cream and short-order meals. Residents met at a few tables to discuss local affairs while having a quick breakfast or lunch.

The town called Lakeville does not have any lakes. It has a dozen ponds, three of which are large enough but not deep enough to be lakes. The fishing is good in the ponds and streams. Lakeville had two public golf courses and one private 9-hole course on the private Rotch estate. Lydia Rotch, a single lady, lived on the Rotch estate located between Long Pond and Highland Rd. in the "Hill Top Farm" on Highland Rd, where she maintained many horses and provided instruction and riding on trails in the estate. It had a couple of small cottages for her maintenance staff.

The estate also had a large "Stonehouse" where she previously lived with her family. It is located on Apponequet Drive, a private winding dirt road off Highland Rd. This house had an adjoining Horse stable and a large Guest House further up a winding hill that was surrounded by her private 9-hole golf course. This is where Ted would live when he began living full-time during the summers beginning in 1961.

Lydia was a very talented woman. Artistic, sculptor, athletic, and a pilot owning her own plane. She was also a Red Sox fan. Ted and Lydia would become close friends.

All of this is to let you, the reader, understand that Ted was going to feel comfortable in this environment, just as he was in 1938 when playing for the Minneapolis Millers in Princeton, Minnesota. Princeton was a rural town of similar size with good fishing and hunting and down-to-earth, friendly residents. This is where he returned for a winter vacation in his shiny new Buick Convertable after his first years playing professional baseball in Boston. He wanted to be with "regular" friendly people in his off-season time. There, he could relax. He felt he could now relax in Lakeville.

On arrival in Lakeville, Ted greeted Albert with his common greeting, "Hiya Sport" at the "Wife and I" Convenience Store. Before Al could begin his promotion, Ted asked. "How's the fishing here?" Al pointed out the large pond across the street and added that there were many other ponds and streams in the town, including Loon Pond on the Boy Scout property. This was his opener. They sat down at one of the tables and were waited on by a local gal, ordering coffee and locally made pastry.

Al explained his problem obtaining a mortgage from a local bank. The property had all the essentials needed for a large Boys' Baseball Camp, but the bank declined his requests on two occasions.

His lack of funds and their decision that it would be too much of a business risk without a prominent sports figure who would also provide the necessary financial support. One previous attempt had the support of recently retired heavyweight boxer Rocky Marciano. The bank didn't

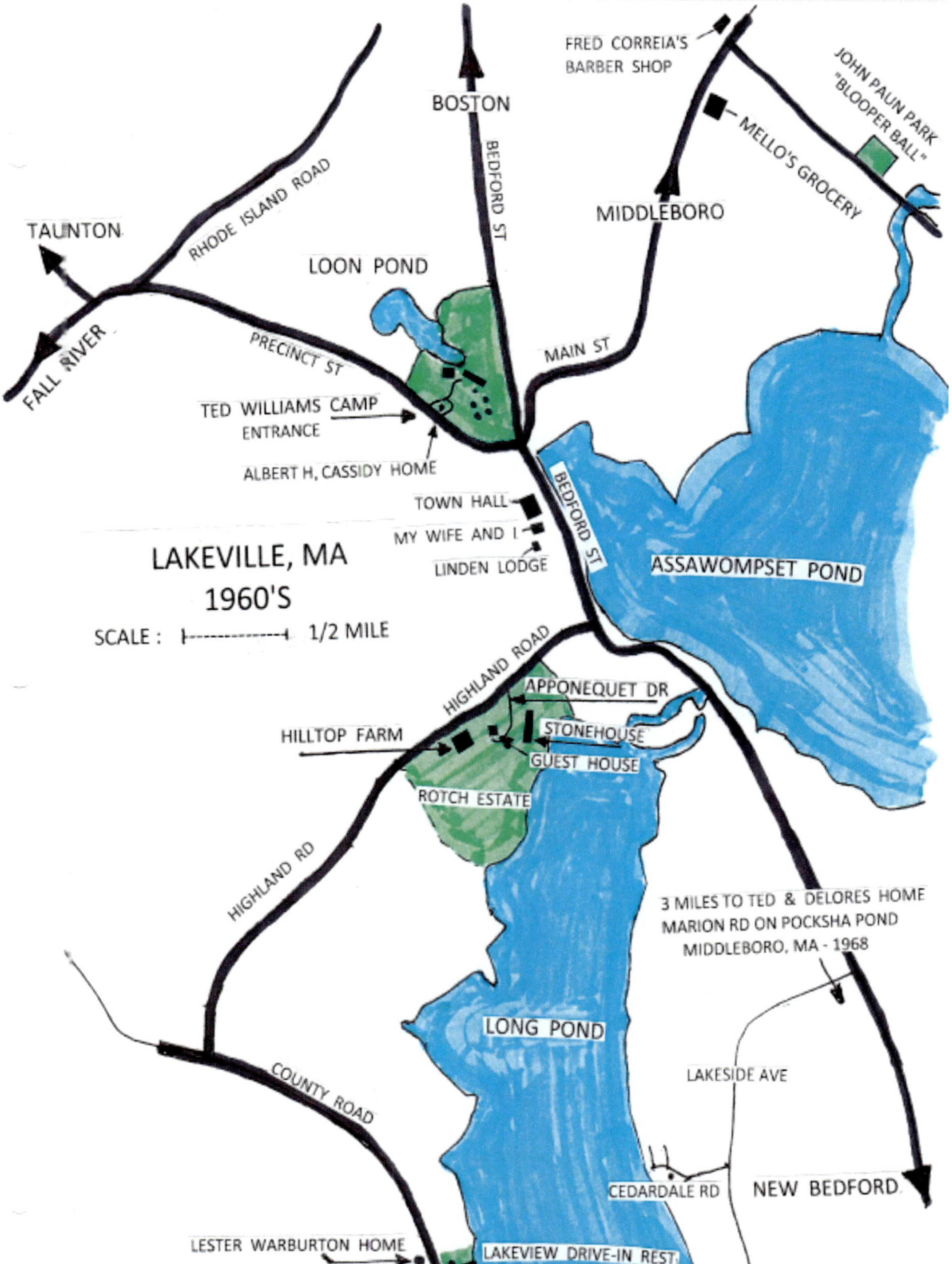
FRED CORREIA'S BARBER SHOP
BOSTON
BEDFORD ST
JOHN PAUN PARK "BLOOPER BALL"
MELLO'S GROCERY
MIDDLEBORO
RHODE ISLAND ROAD
TAUNTON
LOON POND
FALL RIVER
PRECINCT ST
MAIN ST
TED WILLIAMS CAMP ENTRANCE
ALBERT H. CASSIDY HOME
TOWN HALL
MY WIFE AND I
LINDEN LODGE
BEDFORD ST
ASSAWOMPSET POND
LAKEVILLE, MA
1960'S
SCALE : 1/2 MILE
HIGHLAND ROAD
APPONEQUET DR
HILLTOP FARM
STONEHOUSE
GUEST HOUSE
ROTCH ESTATE
HIGHLAND RD
3 MILES TO TED & DELORES HOME
MARION RD ON POCKSHA POND
MIDDLEBORO, MA - 1968
LONG POND
LAKESIDE AVE
COUNTY ROAD
CEDARDALE RD
NEW BEDFORD
LESTER WARBURTON HOME
BERNIE CASSIDY HOME
ALBERT CASSIDY HOME
LAKEVIEW DRIVE-IN REST.
CASSIDY LANE
BUB'S MARINE

think a boxer should be involved with a baseball venture. Who wanted their kid to come home with a broken nose?

Al had photos and made a well-prepared, optimistic presentation. They then left in Teds Cadilac Convertable and drove less than one mile to the entrance of the Scout Camp. After driving through a short wooded area, they viewed a large multi-acre grassed area with a couple of baseball diamonds and room for the many tents where Scouts from the Boston area slept. They parked above the Scout centre of Activity overlooking Loon Pond.

TED WAS IMMEDIATELY IMPRESSED

Al then suggested they drive to his Drive-In restaurant for lunch 5 miles away, still in Lakeville. The drive went past the Rotch estate on Highland Rd. Al explained who the Rotches were and their prominence in the Lakeville community.

When they arrived, Ted was introduced to Al's brother Bernie, who was running the Lakeview Drive-In restaurant. Ted was introduced to Lester Warburton, the husband of Al and Bernie's sister Ethel.

It was evident that they were a close-knit, happy extended family, all about Ted's age. They all participated in the Cassidy businesses. They lived next to each other on the edge of Long Pond, next to the Drive-In restaurant and next door to Bub's Marine. Al and Bernie lived on the short street "Cassidy Lane," leading down to a dock on the pond. Bub's was the major supplier of boating equipment and where fishermen parked or rented boats. Long Pond was one mile wide and stretched north to south, two miles in each direction. Good fishing!

TED WAS FURTHER IMPRESSED

It was apparent that the three partners worked well together. Al, Bernie and Lester were about 40 years old, the same age as Ted. They were active sports enthusiasts and involved with town activities. Two drove school buses. One was a part-time police officer. Bernie was a decorated veteran of World War II and served under General George Patton in the Battle of the Buldge. Their wives were involved with the business, and each of them had children of camping age.

Along with Ted, they were looking forward to a new business experience. Ted spent the night with the Cassidys, enjoying each other's company. They had a lot in common.

Ted spent the night pondering his situation and the opportunity presenting itself. He wanted to know more. He was excited. Everything was falling into place quickly.

DECISION MAKING TIME

The following morning, Ted led the discussion, wanting to know more about the need to start such a program. He was drawing from his vast experiences, including travel, which would be required of Campers, and the need for absolute discipline of everyone. Ted's life in the Marines demonstrated the importance of discipline for success. The program was to be very active, well scheduled and, importantly - FUN Baseball would be played every day all week for eight weeks in the months beginning in September and ending in June.

They outlined the need to improve the facilities. Add dormitory housing and add a couple of new ball fields and equipment. Provide additional sports activities such as swimming, boating, fishing, archery, and entertainment during off hours.

Staffing was discussed with the partners, noting that local area public schools would be closed when the camp was active. Teachers, Coaches and Management would be available and looking for paid part-time work. Legal and Medical services would be needed and available. Also, Albert Bernie and Lester would have to dedicate their time throughout the year to organize the program, including recruiting campers locally, mostly from across the country, and even from other countries.

Ted acknowledged that he was prepared to provide all of the advance funding, including these "Partners" salaries. He also clarified that this project was to be done without the public knowledge of his full financial commitment. Also, he would allow his name to be used for the name of the Camp. He still had three years left of baseball in his contract with the Red Sox. He would make himself available during this period, frequently visiting the Camp when possible to oversee the progress expected of the partners and when the Camp was active.

The partners all agreed with the results of these meetings, which lasted another day. It was agreed that they first had to purchase the Boy Scout Camp. It was left up to Albert to visit the local bank in Middleboro again with the good news that he had secured the approval of Ted Williams to back the project financially and that the camp would be named "Ted Williams Boys Baseball Camp." Ted returned to his suite at the Boston hotel.

Albert visited the local bank again with the good news. They questioned Ted's agreement to be the sponsor. A phone call was made and Ted answered with the confirmation that he would support the creation of a boy's baseball camp. The Bank was still unconvinced that the camp would be successful and again turned down the request for a mortgage.

Al and Ted talked again on the phone following the meeting. Ted said he would contact someone he knew of at the Middleboro Co-Operative Bank and get back to Al.

Ted was able to talk to an official of the Co-Op Bank and explain the situation. A meeting was set for the next day, and Ted and Albert met in person at the bank with the bank's voting members. They were impressed and formally agreed to take the mortgage.

Ted wrote out a check for $12,000 to cover the mortgage's 20% deposit. At the same meeting, Ted and Al opened a checking account, and Ted made a substantial deposit to cover the anticipated expenses.

Ted and Al then went to Al's Lakeview Drive-In to meet with Bernie and Lester.

Ted made it clear that he was fully in support of establishing a baseball camp and expected that they would do the same. All major decisions were to be made above board; nothing hidden! They shook hands on this and toasted the new partnership with Coffee Frappes. They were not alcohol drinkers and none was available at the Drive-In restaurant.

Albert was voted as the Executive Director of "Ted Williams Boys Baseball Camp Inc." Bernard Cassidy was named as Clerk of the Board of Directors. Ted gave each of them a 25% share in the business, and he held the other 25%. They hired a lawyer and officially Incorporated the partnership. When the deed was recorded at the Plymouth County Registry of Deeds on December 10, 1957, Albert H. Cassidy was listed as the owner. Ted Williams's name does not appear on the Deed. Much planning had been done before the formal recording of the deed.

TED WAS ENSURING THAT THIS PROJECT WAS FOR THE PURPOSE OF HELPING YOUNG BOYS BECOME DISCIPLINED MEN WITH CHARACTER, WHATEVER THEIR FUTURE WAS TO BE. HE WAS ADAMANT THAT HE WAS GIVING OF HIMSELF FOR OTHERS - NOT FOR HIMSELF. THUS THIS "LEGACY WAS OVERLOOKED" BY THE PRESS AND THE PUBLIC UNTIL NOW.

The mortgage was signed. There would be a few weeks before physical changes to the property could be made when the Deed was recorded. There was, however, a massive amount of work to be done in the meantime. The Partners would make a list and responsibilities to establish a Camp they wished could begin the following June.

Here is a sample of a list:

- Allocate each other's Responsibilities
- Define additional Activities to be supported.
- Swimming, Boating, Fishing, Tennis, Archery, Horseback Riding
- Support a Girl's Day Camp on Loon Pond
- Hire full-time help - Legal, Organizational, Secretarial, Financial, Medical
- Rent Office Space with Phone and Teletype Service
- Define physical Camp needs
- Layout the new Camp facilities
- Build two new Baseball Diamonds
- Improve and expand Dinning Hall facilities
- Create Housing for 125 boys ages 7-18
- Create Housing for Staff coming from away
- Install Electric Power and Plumbing facilities including Toilets, Lighting, Public

Address
- Add a Laundry
- Add Outhouses
- Add Storage facilities for Equipment and Supplies
- Define the daily routine for training and playing baseball
- Define Additional Training for Campers in Other Activities
- Find activities for Weekends
- Define Transportation needs Daily and Weekends
- Order Uniforms - Contract with local Sports Supplier

Note: Albert H. Cassidy and Bernard J Cassidy are the sons of Albert Cassidy Jr

1956 Tax records:	Albert Cassidy Jr,	age 63	Paid $150 RE Tax
	Albert H.	age 40	No Tax (Lived with father)
	Bernard J	age 39	Paid $102 RE Tax
	* Les Warburton,	age 37	Paid $ 503 RE Tax
	Arthur G. Rotch		Paid $1937 RE Tax
	Boy Scout Camp		No Tax found

* Note: The family jointly owned a long stretch of property along County Street, with the Warburtons living in a large older home at the northern end of the property, who were listed as the owners, thus paying the high tax. The families were typical of the area and had an entrepreneurial spirit. Al is quoted as telling his children that "American" is spelt with the last four letters - "I CAN."

This is the environment that Ted met on the day he visited Lakeville.

Ted was comfortable with the area and the "regular" people he met.

The following few days were spent discussing details about funding, organizing, and staffing a Boys Baseball Camp, including a Camp for Girls. All the fundamentals were there.

The property was well established in size, with a pond and many existing facilities that could be used, including an office building and a few small cottages that would accommodate staff. Other small buildings existed for equipment storage and for arts and crafts. A large level grassed area had two baseball fields, and campers used the area for their tents. There was room for additional ball fields.

The plan to open only in the summer months meant that the area public school systems would be closed, and their staff would be looking for summer employment. They would have all the necessary talents required to efficiently run a camp for boys and girls of all ages. Coaches- Counselors- Educators - Nurses - Organizers - Facility Maintenance - Busses and Drivers, experienced and affordable. The Cassidys had the ability and desire to head up the experiment by endorsing a wealthy, interested, and notable baseball hero who would be a drawing card for potential Campers from around the USA and even foreign countries. What was missing? - A bank

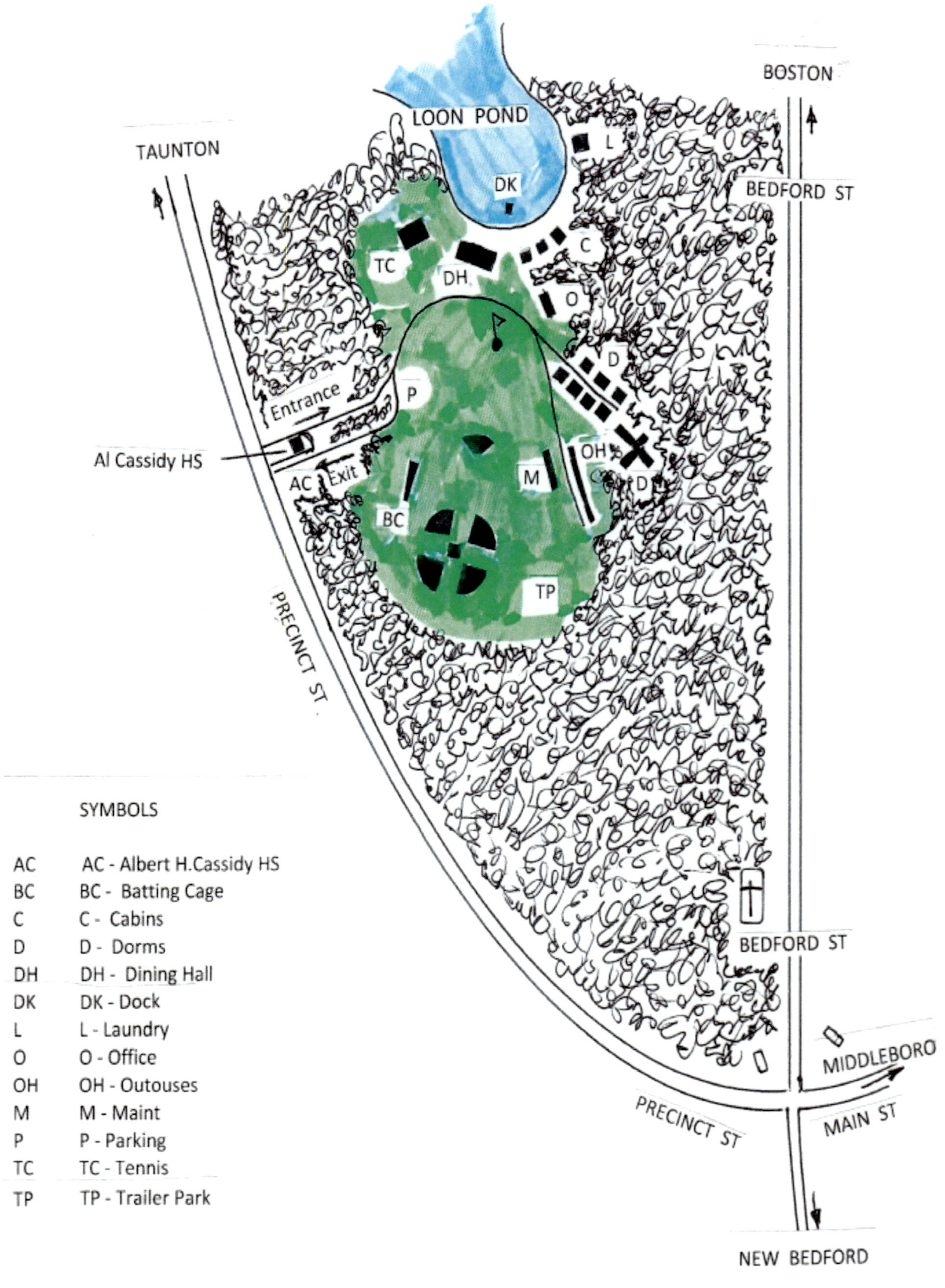
LOON POND
TAUNTON
BOSTON
BEDFORD ST
L
DK
C
TC
DH
O
D
P
Entrance
Al Cassidy HS
AC
Exit
OH
M
D
BC
TP
PRECINCT ST
BEDFORD ST
MIDDLEBORO
MAIN ST
PRECINCT ST
NEW BEDFORD
SYMBOLS
AC AC - Albert H.Cassidy HS
BC BC - Batting Cage
C C - Cabins
D D - Dorms
DH DH - Dining Hall
DK DK - Dock
L L - Laundry
O O - Office
OH OH - Outouses
M M - Maint
P P - Parking
TC TC - Tennis
TP TP - Trailer Park

Boston Council, Inc., Boy Scouts of America, the holder of a mortgage by Albert H. Cassidy and others to it, said Boston Council, Inc., Boy Scouts of America, dated January 13, 1958, recorded with Plymouth County Registry of Deeds, Book 2613, Page 69, for consideration paid, release to Albert H. Cassidy, all interest acquired under said mortgage in the following described portions of the mortgaged premises

The land in Lakeville, Plymouth County, Massachusetts on the Northerly side of the Taunton Road known as Precinct Street, also as laid out by the County Commissioners by their Decree No. 656 and shown on Plan, March 22, 1936, Lewis W. Perkins, County Engineer, bounded and described as follows: Beginning at a point in the Northerly line of said Street, at an intermediate Plymouth County Bound situated 973.885 feet Northwest as measured in the line of said Street from a Plymouth County Bound marking the Northwesterly end of a curve shown on said plan having a radius of 980.00 Feet and an arc of 636.97 feet; thence North 29° 15' West in line of said Street 32 feet; thence North 60° 45' East 80 feet; thence North 29° 15' West 25 feet; thence North 60° 45' East 80 feet; thence South 29° 15' East 168 feet; thence South 60° 45' West 160 feet to the Northerly line of said Street; thence in said line North 29° 15' West 111 feet to the bound first mentioned as surveyed by Henry L. Pember, November 1958.

Together with the right to pass and repass to and from said premises and said Street over the driveway as now used over an area 80 feet in length and 25 feet in width contiguous to and Northwesterly from the line hereinbefore described as running North 60° 45' East 80 feet from Precinct Street and Southwesterly of and contiguous to the line hereinbefore described as North 29° 15' West 25 feet.

In witness whereof the said Boston Council, Inc., Boy Scouts of America has caused a common seal to be hereto affixed and these presents to be signed, in its name and behalf by Elliott Henderson, its president and Philip Dean its treasurer this fifth day of January A. D. 1959, said corporation having no corporate seal.

Boston Council, Inc., Boy Scouts of America

by Elliott Henderson President

by Philip Dean Treasurer

Book 267
Pg 350
Jan 5, 1959

willing to take the $60,000 mortgage from an inexperienced party.

The cooperative bank had readily agreed to take the mortgage. Ted's name does not appear on the Deed to the property; He intentionally kept his name out of the public spotlight. This was to be something he wanted to do without his name again gaining notoriety. He didn't want the Boston Press writing articles to sell more papers. Oh! How would they be compensated? They would have to adjust their own business and personal affairs.

The three partners worked together overtime from October 1957 to June 1958

- only 8 months - when an Open House was scheduled to be held. The Camp was to begin its first year late in June 1958.

They did the following: (and more!)

- Design, contract, and build a Dormitory to house up to 75 young boys, their counselors, and staff families.
- Design and build additional smaller dormitories for older Campers and their

Coaches
- Double the size of the existing dining hall, referred to as Loon Lodge
- Add three baseball diamonds, five batting cages, five dugouts, and fencing.
- Add suitable suitable seating for spectators
- Provide two Pitching/Catching training paths
- Build an on-site laundry
- Advertise nationally for boys ages 7-18 to attend a live-in Camp for up to (4) two week sessions during the months of June, July, and August 1958. Cost - $125 per Camper for each 2 week session.
- Order uniforms for each of the three age groups - 7-10, 11 to 15, and 16-18.
- Order equipment. Bats, Balls, Gloves, etc., pitching machine, bases for the five baseball diamonds, towels, etc.?
- Order and install Loud Speaker System, Electrical, including Lighting and Plumbing systems
- Provide service for laundry cleaning - every day
- provide sanitary toilet facilities for boys and Girls
- Hire specialized talents in finance, secretarial, legal, etc.
- Provide Security 24/7 from June through August
- Assure attendance 24/7 - Roll Call/ Flag raising/Pledge of Allegiance
- Provide transportation to church services
- Contact and commit necessary talents from local schools – Coaches, Counselors, Administrators, Nurses, Chefs, Bus Drivers etc?
- Coordinate with town officials regarding necessary agreements.
- Keep Ted advised
- Obtain Ted's funding as needed.
- Meet with Ted to get his continued advice on how he envisioned the Operation of the Camp, Scheduled activities and discipline, his presence and involvement, etc.

The first year was the learning year, with adjustments made as needed. It was not a for-profit operation for the first few years. Ted did not take any money from the operation. He paid the bills as needed out of his own pocket. The Camp operated this way until Ted retired from the Red Sox in 1960

Ted made frequent visits at appropriate times from 1957 through 1960. He was present for an Open House on June 2 and the Opening Day on June 28, 1958

2024 - J & J SEAFOOD RESTAURANT County Road, Lakeville , MA

Site of old Cassidy's
Drive-in- Restaurant
1957
view from corner of
Cassidy Lane &
County Road

Todays Drive-Up window
J & J Seafood Restaurant

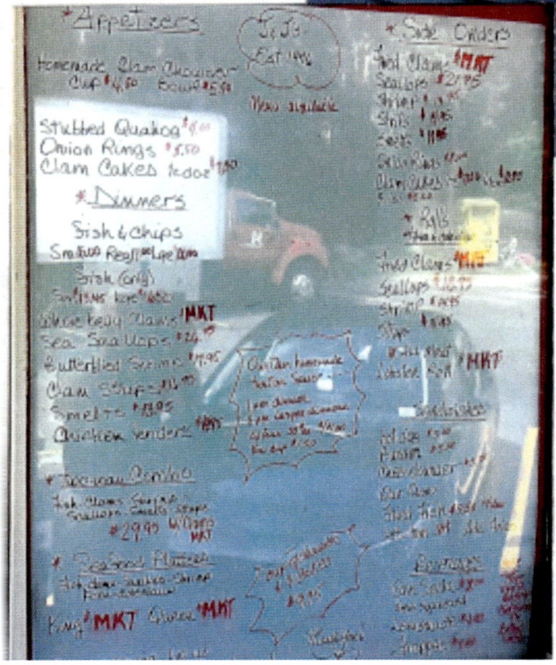

J & J's Saefood Menue
June 2024

Note: Top of Menue

J&J's
Est. 1976

1957 Lakeview Drive-in-restaurant now known as J & J Restaurant 1976-2024

Cassidy's Lakeview
Drive-in- Restaurant
1957
view from corner of
Cassidy Lane &
County Road

Cassidy's Lakeview
Drive-in- Restaurant
looking toward
Bub's Marine on
Cassidy Lane

Location of (2)
Cassidy Homes
1957
Albert &
son Albert H.
& family
Son Bernard
& family

BUB'S MARINE
on Cassidy Lane
cr. of County Road
Long Pond in
background

TED'S PERSONAL LIFE CONTINUED TO BE ACTIVE - VERY ACTIVE

CHAPTER: 10

TED WILLIAMS BOYS BASEBALL CAMP BEGINS 1958

The Opening Day Ceremony is best told by the writer of the local Middleboro Gazette printed on Wednesday, June 5th, 1958, following the Monday event - June 3.

"TED WILLIAMS AT CAMP OPENING "

300 Attend Ceremony At Loon Pond Site

> An estimated 300 persons, at least half of them baseball-minded youngsters, were at hand at the Ted Williams Baseball Camp in Lakeville when its famous name sake appeared to attend the official opening Monday.
>
> Ted Williams was accompanied by former Red Sox teammate Eddie Pelligrini, now coaching college baseball, and with him and camp directors and owners, formed a receiving line to greet the visitors. Included in the line was Al Cassidy, executive director; Fred Cassidy, camp director; Bernard Cassidy and Lester Warburton, co-owners with Ted. As he met campers who will attend the camp when its activities program gets underway on Friday, June 28. Williams autographed baseballs, camp folders, and photographs, some of the later for enterprising fans who had taken pictures on the spot with Polaroid cameras.
>
> Later, demonstrating a new mechanical pitching machine, he knocked balls into the field and autographed them for the boys who caught them. The machine supplied to the camp by Steve Stanley, a local sports equipment dealer, is an improvement over previous types in that it duplicates the motion of a pitcher's arm instead of firing practice pitches in the manner of a gun.
>
> Williams also conferred with Chester Sylvester, a local plumbing contractor, on the camp's sanitary facilities, which will provide living quarters for some 150 campers. His inspection tour was critical and complete, and when he was finished, he said he was pleased with the setup.
>
> Much of his time was taken up posing for newspaper and TV cameramen with visitors, camp officials and a band made up of newspaper boys from New Bedford. Taunton radio station WPEP made a live broadcast, and others taped the ceremonies for rebroadcast.
>
> Lakeville town officials who attended the opening included Selectmen Wallace C. Wilkie, chairman Harry Norris, and Ralph Baker. Police Chief John S. Erwin and patrolmen Michael Brienzo and Nelson Sherman. Mrs. Evelyn Norris, town

clerk; Mrs. Phyilis Draghetti, selectman's clerk; and Mrs. Lubelle Martin. Manuel J. Silvia, chairman of the Middleboro Board of Selectmen, and Stephen Horbal, Gas & Electric Department manager, attended.

Helen Robins, fish warden, presented Williams with a fishing license."

Note: No record was found in the Taunton Daily Gazette or the New Bedford Standard-Times newspapers of the Ted Williams Boys Baseball Camp Opening Ceremony on June 3 or the opening of the Camp beginning Friday, June 28, when some of the Campers arrived, through Monday, July 1, when the first activities began.

BASEBALL BASICS

by Ted Williams

TED WILLIAMS BASEBALL CAMP

LAKEVILLE, MA 02346
TEL. 617-947-0726

But the following article was found: the New Bedford Standard-Times reported an unfortunate accident - Page 1 July 4th when a 15-year-old boy was reported drowned in Loon Pond in Lakeville.

No mention was made if he was a Boy's Baseball Camper, even though he died on the afternoon of July 3 during the first week of camp operations. He was observed swimming toward and holding onto a rowboat by a lady sitting on her porch facing the pond, but there was no cry for help. He lived in East Taunton on Middleboro Ave. and would not have been an "Over-Night" Camper.

Camp operations included boating and life-saving instruction on the shore of Loon Pond during weekdays all summer. Was it active during the 4th of July week?

The Camp Management certainly was aware that Campers were exposed to all kinds of injuries and their liability to them. They were always staffed with qualified personnel to prevent such an accident.

The Newspaper commented, "It marred the opening of what was promised to be a busy holiday weekend at Southeastern Mass and Cape Cod."

(This is not a very detailed explanation embedded in a long report of the busy 4th of July vacation traffic. ???????)

By 1957, Ted had a full life, and in addition to his full commitment to supporting the new boys' camp, he had met and became attached to Isabel Gilmore, who was divorced and had two young sons, Marshall and Grant. He sent them to his Boys Baseball Camp. They lasted only two weeks. No interest in baseball. Ted was romantic yet demanding of her full commitment. He proposed marriage and was turned down in 1958. Ted did not want to be tied down to nurturing a family. She wanted him to do this. She was taken by his positive, loving, and romantic personality, and they stayed friends throughout his life.

In 1958, Ted was invited to become a member of the exclusive Miramichi Anglers. Association with a large Lodge on the Miramichi River in Gray Rapids, New BrunswickCanada. He visited the Lodge and became friendly with a required local guide, Roy Curtis. He asked Roy to find him an ideal parcel of land on the river's edge where he could build his own lodge.

The first day of the first year of the newly created "Ted Williams Boys Baseball Camp. The camp was on Friday, June 28, 1958. This was when young boys were beginning to be picked up at rail stations, bus stations, and airports coming from around the USA. They needed to be greeted and acclimated to their new environment. Boys from Lakeville, those from the surrounding towns, and those being driven to Lakeville by their parents would arrive on Saturday and join the others already there. Formal greetings and orientation for an estimated 125 Campers were expected. This was the limit set by the owners. A very successful beginning.

MEET TED WILLIAMS... BASEBALL'S SUPERSTAR

Ted Williams is known to baseball fans as the most spectacular hitter in the past 30 years... the last of the 400 hitters! Elected to Baseball's Hall of Fame by the widest margin ever given to a major leaguer, Ted is the only baseball player to have batted over 400 since 1941. Ted won the League's Batting Champion 6 times. He was twice voted the League's most valuable player and was voted the player of the Decade in 1950 by Veteran Players and Sports Writers. He played in 18 All-Star games and has a lifetime total of 2,654 base hits, ending his active playing days with a .344 average.

- **Ted Williams was elected to baseball's Hall of Fame in 1966 by the greatest margin ever accorded a major leaguer.**
- **Even though his career was twice interrupted by military service, he was voted Player of the Decade in 1950.**
- **Ted Williams was the last major leaguer to hit over .400 in a season since 1941 when he hit 406.**
- **Ted William's lifetime batting average is .344 with a total of 2.654 base hits.**

Orientation answered many questions and set the standard for their future at Camp. Each Camper was given a 6" x 8" booklet entitled "BASEBALL BASICS by Ted Williams - Ted Williams Baseball Camp Lakeville, MA 02346 Tel. 617-947-0726".

They were instructed to read it and use it for reference throughout their session.

All young campers were required to have proper haircuts, a military discipline expected by Ted Williams at the beginning of their experience. Ted recruited his barber and friend, Fred Correia, to set up shop at the Camp periodically to implement this from the beginning. Ted was known to send a young camper to see Fred with the demand, "You need a haircut!"

The enrollment charge this first year was $125 for each of the four 2 week sessions, $250 for four weeks and $490 for those who would attend the whole eight weeks.

This was a lot of money for the average family to pay. Yet many families stretched their budgets, realizing that this would be a rewarding experience for their son in the presence of the highly regarded Ted Williams. Albert H. Cassidy did an outstanding job recruiting a full complement of Campers for this first year.

HOW TO BE A BETTER HITTER

"Thousands of words have been written about the business of hitting a baseball. The art of putting the 'fat of the bat' on the ball at the right instant has been studied by expert coaches and outstanding players ever since the game began. What I have to say here is the result of my own experiences in baseball as a player and as a Manager of a major league team. Hitting has been my chief interest in baseball since I began to play as a boy in grade school. I like to hit and other than winning a game, a good solid base hit was always the most thrilling experience in playing baseball. I believe that I have worked as hard and practiced as much to improve my hitting as any player I've known. Yet, if I had to do it over again, I'd probably practice hitting even more than I did! While hitting depends on practice more than any other factor there are some basic fundamentals to be learned. We hope this book gives you a better understanding of these fundamentals and helps you get those base hits more often."

Good Luck!

Ted Williams

The sessions were scheduled for the weekend before baseball training started on Monday. This was a first for everybody. The town of Lakeville had never seen such a busy day in its rural quiet center, which would continue for 8-10 weeks every summer until 1986.

Discipline was enacted immediately in support of Ted's demands. Reveille awakened the boys on the outside loudspeaker system at 6 am. The "Yellow Shirt" Counselors sleeping in the same quarters with each age group in their separate dormitories (barracks ?) made sure their boys were standing at attention when the United States flag was raised outside their quarters and the National Anthem was broadcast.

Then they rush to the dining hall for their first buffet breakfast. A few of the staff serving the breakfast were "To Be" Campers earning their free Camping experience by serving an equal number of weeks working in the dining room. They were boys who lived in the neighborhood and rode their bikes to the Camp. This was a practical offering by the partners when financial resources were limited, and it filled the need to staff the dining room.

The scheduling of the day's events started by having specific baseball actions practiced at prearranged locations around the open fields. Pitching by a small group was coached from a few pitching mounds. Catching was taught at adjacent locations. Hitting was coached in newly constructed batting cages with the new mechanical pitching machine. The proper sliding technique was coached on a few wood chip-coated strips, hoping to prevent too many scrapes and bruises. Coaches would hit balls to an outfield while being taught how to efficiently catch and throw a ball back to the infield. The same would be taught at another location for fielding infield hits.

Umpire training was added to the schedule. Baseball rules were taught to all Campers at the beginning of a session and expanded during rainy and hot days when time was available. Umpiring was a good alternative for boys who may not have had athletic ability but had the desire to be actively involved. They could now practice this important element of playing ball by actually umpiring during every game played every afternoon each week. Coaches would be there to make constructive corrections or add an explanation when needed. There was a need for four at each game, thus twenty for the five games being played simultaneously.

Each training event would be rotated by an audible instruction on the loudspeaker system after a specific time. A time-out was allowed for a brief rest. At the end of a morning's outing, the boys would be allowed a few minutes to relax before attending their lunch break. The afternoons were dedicated to playing the game of baseball. That meant that about a dozen boys were assigned to a given team, mainly by age group.

Thus twenty-four boys would be assigned to each of the five fields. There were two major league fields, two Minor league fields, and one Little league field. Thus, all 125 Campers would play ball at the same time. The "Yellow Shirt" counselors kept an accurate record of each boy and their abilities and attention under their watch. After a few days, it would be apparent what boys advanced in the required skills and adjustments would be made to make up new teams of like abilities, thus creating a motivational quality to the camping experience. At all times, it was the job of coaches and counselors to make the experience - FUN.

MAKE THE STRIKE ZONE WORK FOR YOU

STRIKE ZONE

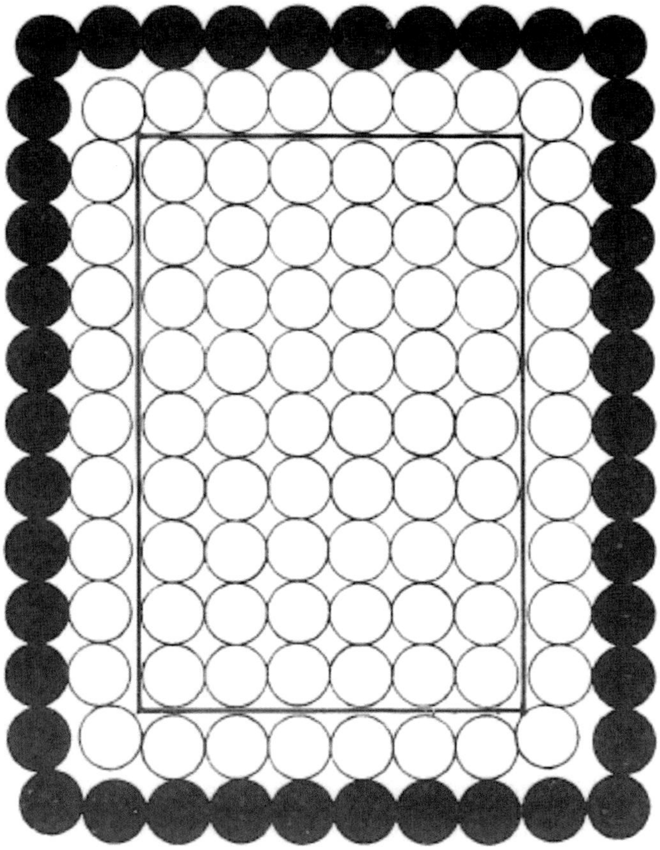

LEARN YOUR HOT ZONE

While home plate is always 17 inches wide the strike zone is roughly 23 inches wide when you consider catching the corners with the ball which is 3¼ inches wide. The height of the strike zone varies with each batter. The rule defines it as the distance from the armpits to the middle of the knee. Judging the strike zone is one of the most important elements of batting. Don't go for balls outside of it. Each player has his own "Hot Zone"—the area within the strike zone where he hits the best. Keep a "book" on yourself. Learn your weaknesses, and your strong points . . . whether you do a better job of hitting balls below the waist or above it, towards the outside or inside of the plate. Illustration above shows strike zone in terms of white balls.
Shaded balls are outside of the strike zone.

OUTGUESSING THE PITCHER

Batting, in my way of thinking, is both mental and physical combat. You are trying to outguess the pitcher and he is trying to outguess you. One of the primary rules of good hitting is getting a good ball to hit. Visualize a window next to pitcher's head and shoulders and watch the ball come out of this window.

WAIT FOR A GOOD BALL

If you get into the habit of swinging at bad pitches, you'll get nothing else. You have the advantage over the pitcher so take your time and look each pitch over carefully. Don't be afraid to take a walk. They can win ball games.

TAKE THE PITCH, IF . . .

When the pitcher fools you or if the pitch is in a tough spot for you to hit . . . take it, unless you have 2 strikes and the ball looks in the strike zone.

IF COUNT GOES TO 2 STRIKES

If the count goes to two strikes, choke up a little on the bat, sacrificing a bit of power for more bat control. Don't make a conscious effort to guide the ball, but concentrate on hitting it squarely and driving it straight back through the pitcher's box.

MAKE PITCHER THROW *YOUR* PITCH

Whenever you swing at pitches outside your strike zone you give the pitcher a bigger target. When you let the bad ones go by you force the pitcher to throw the kind of pitches you can do your best work with.

DEVELOP QUICK, STRONG HANDS

All good hitters have quick hands and wrists. Certainly this is where part of your power comes from. You can strengthen your hands and wrists by swinging an overweight bat, squeezing a rubber ball, using hand exercisers or doing finger push-ups.

KEEP THE PLATE WELL COVERED

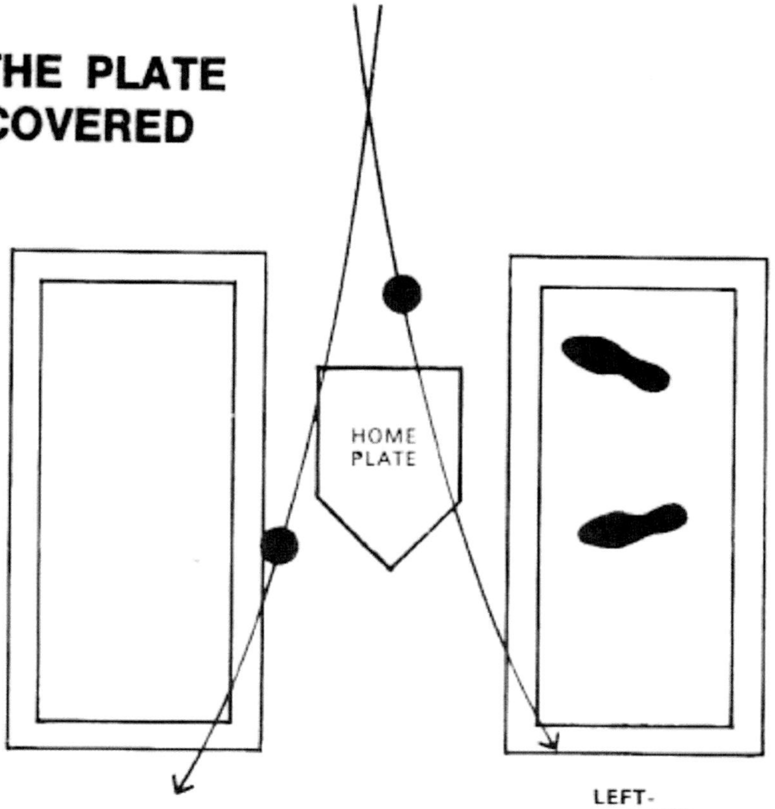

Keep the pitcher's target as small as possible. The further back you stand the bigger strike area you have to cover. It's also tougher to judge whether a ball is catching the corner, and "breaking stuff" breaks bigger if you're too far back. If you crowd the plate you must hit the ball when it's in front of the plate, giving you less time to look at the pitch. This gives the pitcher a better chance of fooling you.

TAKE A FIRM GRIP ON THE BAT

I'm often asked what weight of bat a player should use. My advice is to use the kind of a bat you can handle the best. If you can't get it around fast enough it's too heavy. You are far better off using a bat that is a little too light for you than one that is too heavy. Consider the feel of bat, the size of handle and the weight. They're all important.

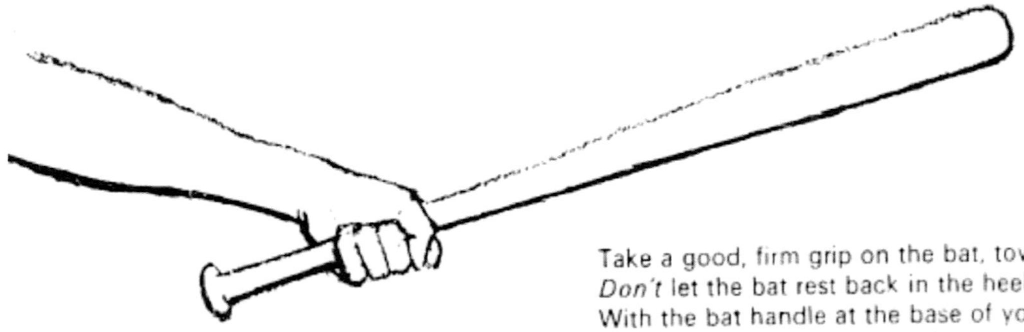

Take a good, firm grip on the bat, toward the fingers. *Don't* let the bat rest back in the heels of your palms. With the bat handle at the base of your fingers, you have much better control.

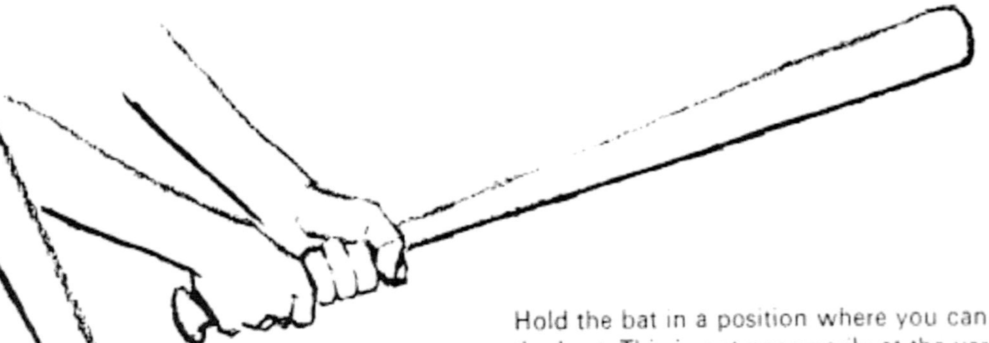

Hold the bat in a position where you can control it the best. This is not necessarily at the very end of the handle. You should have a certain "feel" of the bat that's almost like a part of your own body. Perfect control is the one thing you should strive for.

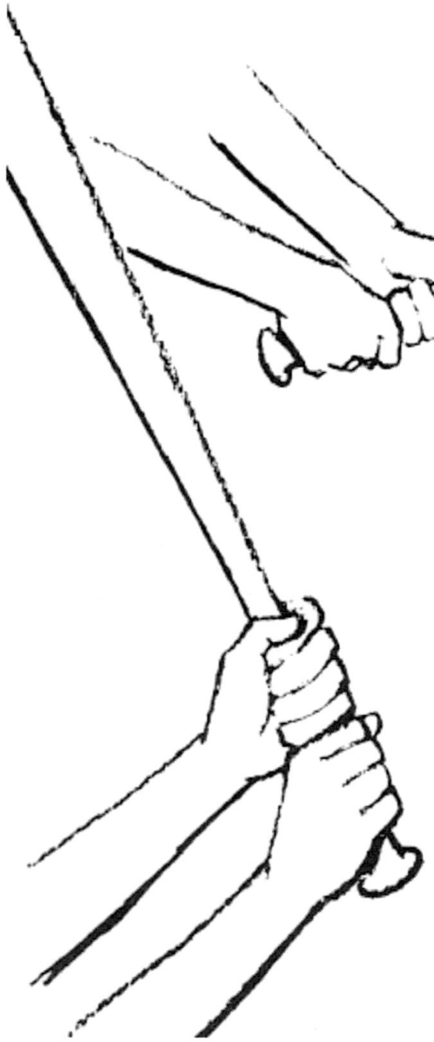

You should have about the same grip on the bat as if you were chopping wood or using a hammer. Index finger should be slightly open. Grip bat firmly *with the fingers* . . . not with the palm.

KEEP YOUR EYE ON THE BALL UNTIL THE LAST INSTANT

One of the most important things about hitting is keeping your eyes on the ball until the last instant. The longer you can wait before you swing at a pitch the better your chances of hitting it squarely. Try to keep your eyes on the ball from the moment the pitcher winds up until you hit it.

TRY TO GET THE FAT PART OF BAT ON CENTER OF BALL

Keep your front shoulder aimed at the pitcher until the start of your swing. Use full power of your hands and wrists, aiming the fat part of the bat at the center of the ball.

To this extent, the partners were very successful. They also had to be aware of any situation that required adjustment before it became a problem. Ted was kept abreast of the process by phone while he was busy playing ball for the Red Sox, traveling to away games. He would visit the Camp when able when the Sox were playing at home.

Weekends required another scheduling situation. As time progressed, the better teams would put on their dress uniforms and either host or travel to another local site to play exhibition games for the public. Again, this was a goal for interested campers and added FUN to their experience.

Other activities were provided for those not selected to play exhibition games.

It was expected that all campers would be instructed in swimming, boating, tennis, horseback riding, archery, and crafts. There was something for everyone at all times. Special trips for educational purposes were planned for those interested. A popular trip was one to Fenway Park when the Red Sox were playing. A few buses were necessary for this trip. Ted was influential in arranging his event.

A special group of seats were sectioned off for his Boys Baseball Campers. They brought their handmade banners (a craft-making product at Camp) and made themselves known to the whole park. Ted would acknowledge them from the batting plate with a tip of his hat and a wave, then proceed to try and place a well-stroked home run ball in their direction. Generally successful!

Once (at least once), a Camper boarded the wrong bus to return home. There were many yellow buses parked in a special parking lot. Other towns had special events for their youth to attend games. The boy would be housed overnight in the other town and be returned the next day to be picked up by a Lakeville volunteer and returned to Camp. The counselor for that boy learned from his mistake that it was his responsibility to know where each of his boys was at all times. The counselor in charge would learn a lesson.

Discipline was required at all times - a Ted Williams requirement.

Once (and only once), a young Camper ventured out into the ball field on a Sunday morning to inspect the new Pitching Machine. He was practicing loading it with baseballs and accidentally hit the ON switch. The mechanical throwing arm hit the boy over the head, cracking his skull. After being rushed to the local St Luke's Hospital in Middleboro then rushed to the other St Luke's Hospital in New Bedford. His condition the next day was listed as "fair." Hopefully, his final recovery was complete. The machine was secured thereafter.

On another occasion, two brothers were missing at the morning Roll Call. two days went by as authorities franticly sought their location, including notification of their parents living in a small town north of Toronto, Canada. At the end of the second day, the brothers arrived home safe and sound. They thumbed their way home.

STANCE AT THE PLATE

Your stance at the plate is something you must determine for yourself. Experiment to find the stance that feels the most comfortable and puts you in a "ready" position. If your stance feels natural and you are getting the "fat" part of the bat on the ball, don't change it. If you are having trouble getting those base hits, these suggestions may be of help.

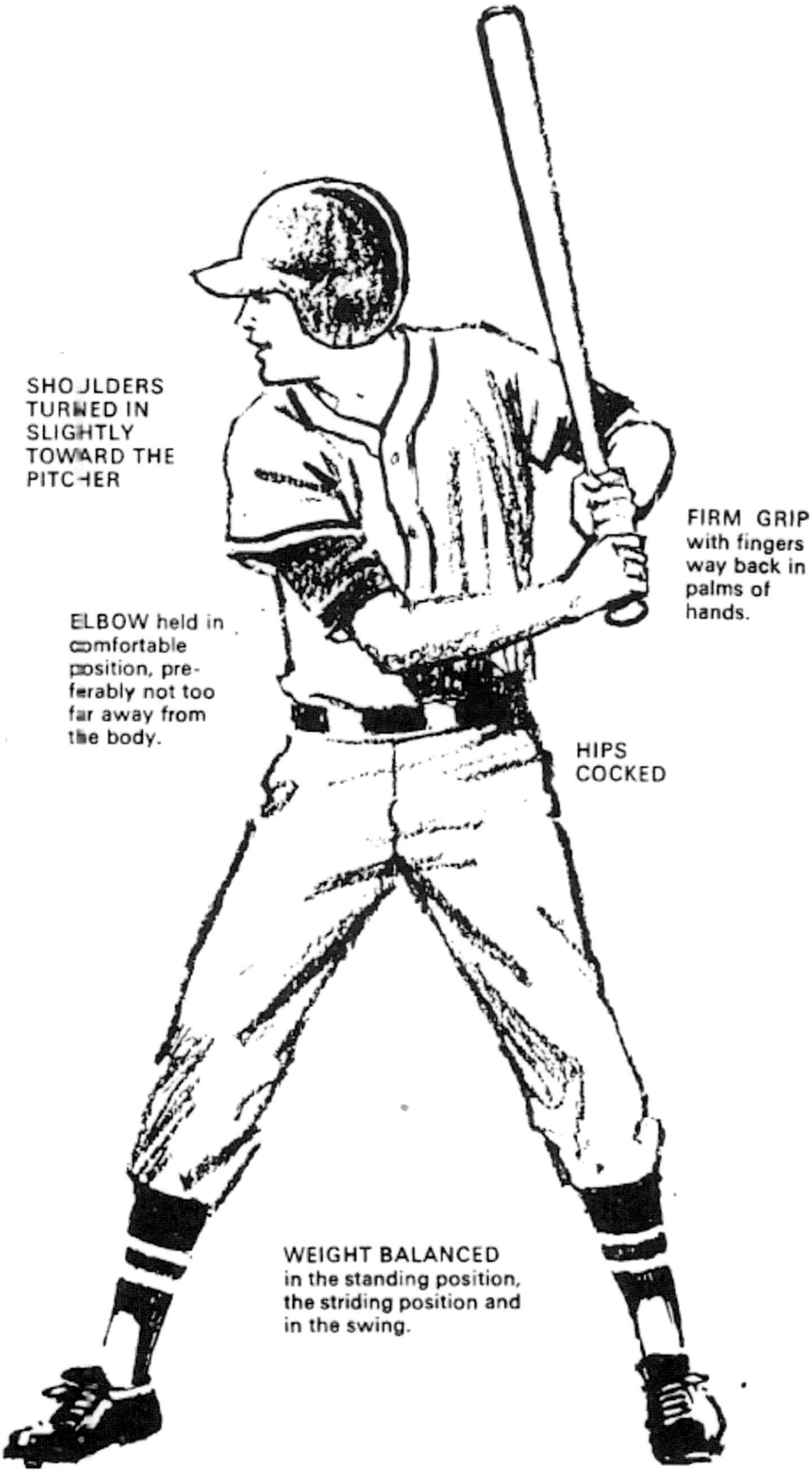

THE SWING'S THE THING

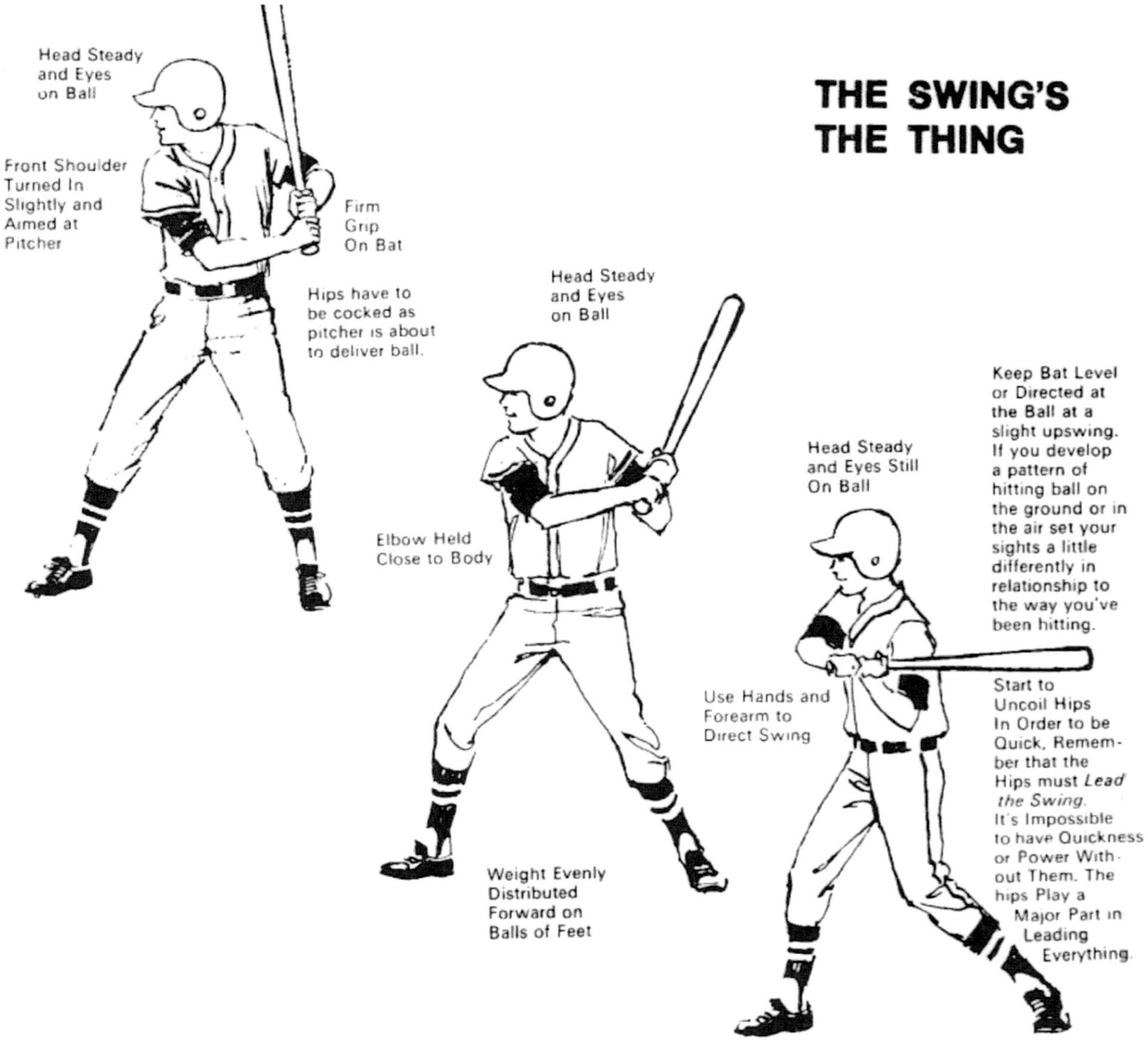

Developing a good swing takes time, patience and practice. Modify these suggestions to suit your own style of batting. There are no hard and fast rules about batting but if you are not hitting the ball good, your swing may need to be polished up.

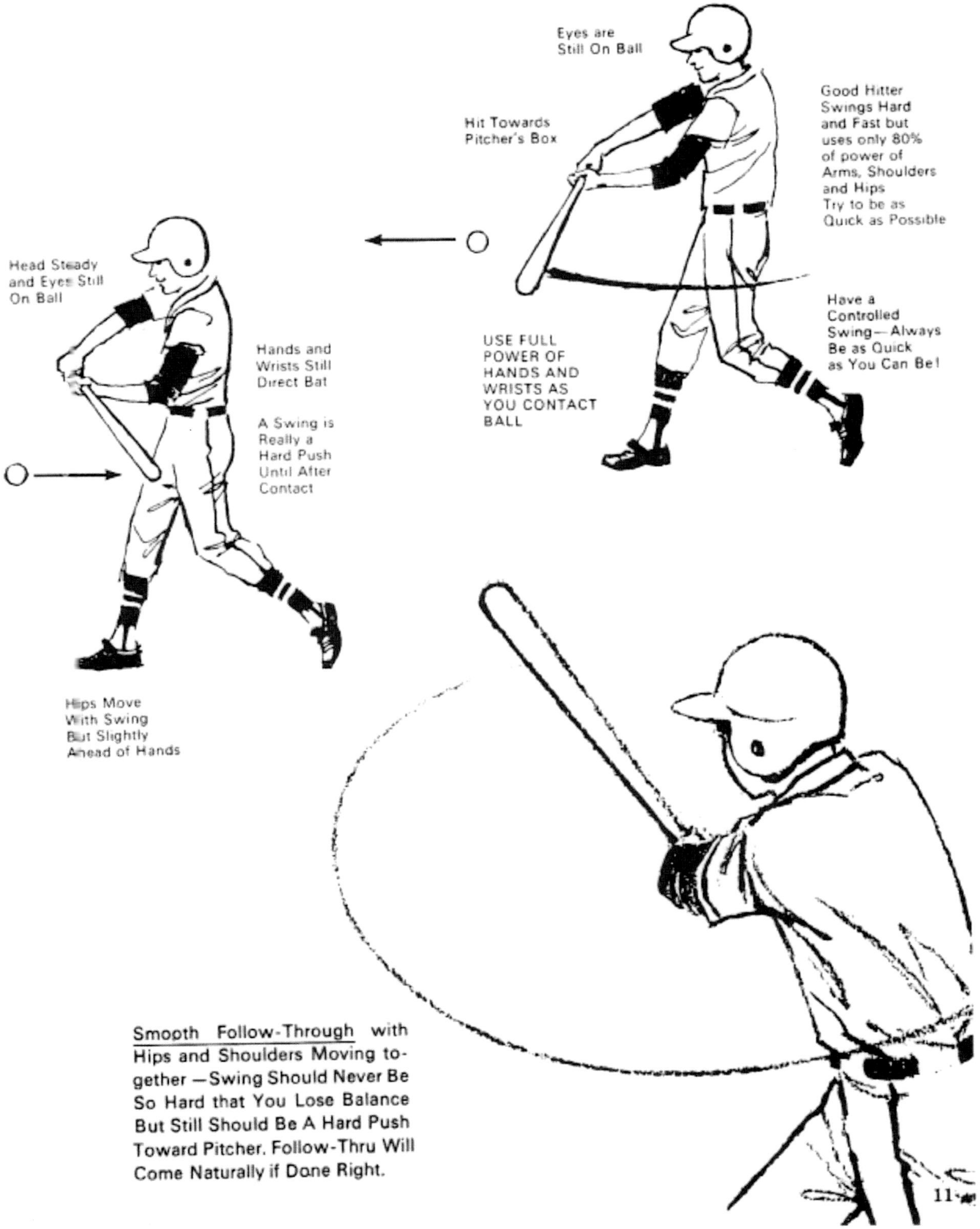
Eyes are Still On Ball
Hit Towards Pitcher's Box
Good Hitter Swings Hard and Fast but uses only 80% of power of Arms, Shoulders and Hips Try to be as Quick as Possible
Have a Controlled Swing—Always Be as Quick as You Can Be!
USE FULL POWER OF HANDS AND WRISTS AS YOU CONTACT BALL
Head Steady and Eyes Still On Ball
Hands and Wrists Still Direct Bat
A Swing is Really a Hard Push Until After Contact
Hips Move With Swing But Slightly Ahead of Hands
Smooth Follow-Through with Hips and Shoulders Moving together—Swing Should Never Be So Hard that You Lose Balance But Still Should Be A Hard Push Toward Pitcher. Follow-Thru Will Come Naturally if Done Right.

FINE POINTS OF BATTING

I don't want to sound like a broken record but practice is the only way I know of to improve your hitting. If you are hitting the ball good . . . practice! If you are in a slump . . . practice! As far as hitting is concerned, practice is the name of the game!

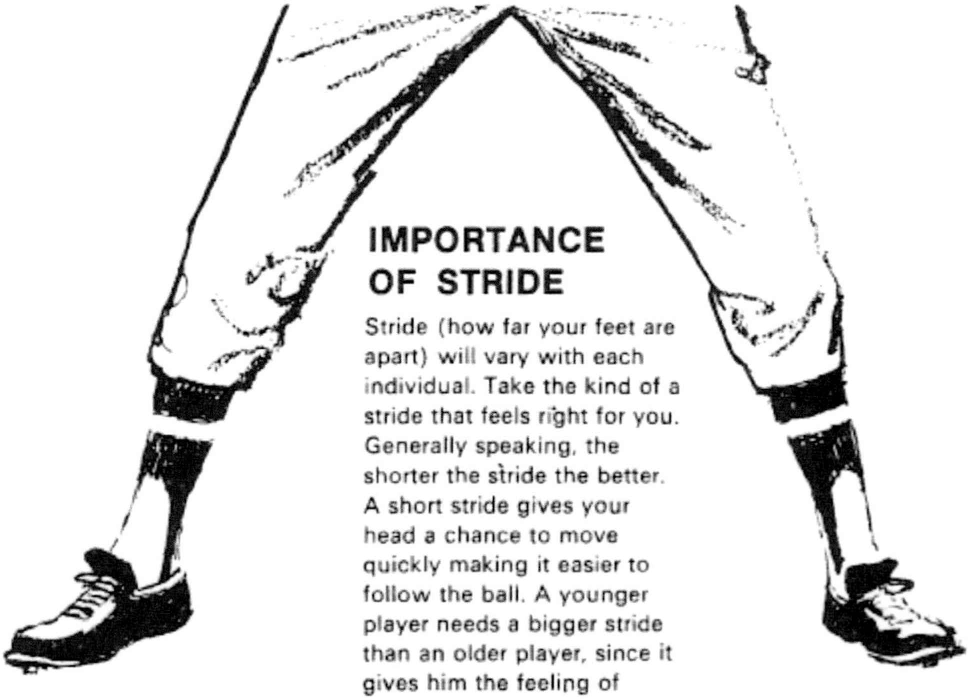

IMPORTANCE OF STRIDE

Stride (how far your feet are apart) will vary with each individual. Take the kind of a stride that feels right for you. Generally speaking, the shorter the stride the better. A short stride gives your head a chance to move quickly making it easier to follow the ball. A younger player needs a bigger stride than an older player, since it gives him the feeling of getting momentum behind his swing.

KEEP HEAD LEVEL

Keep your head level with your eyes on the ball. Let your hands and forearm direct your swing, keeping a firm grip on the bat. Look at ball from an even level. Try cocking your head unnaturally and you'll see how distorts your view.

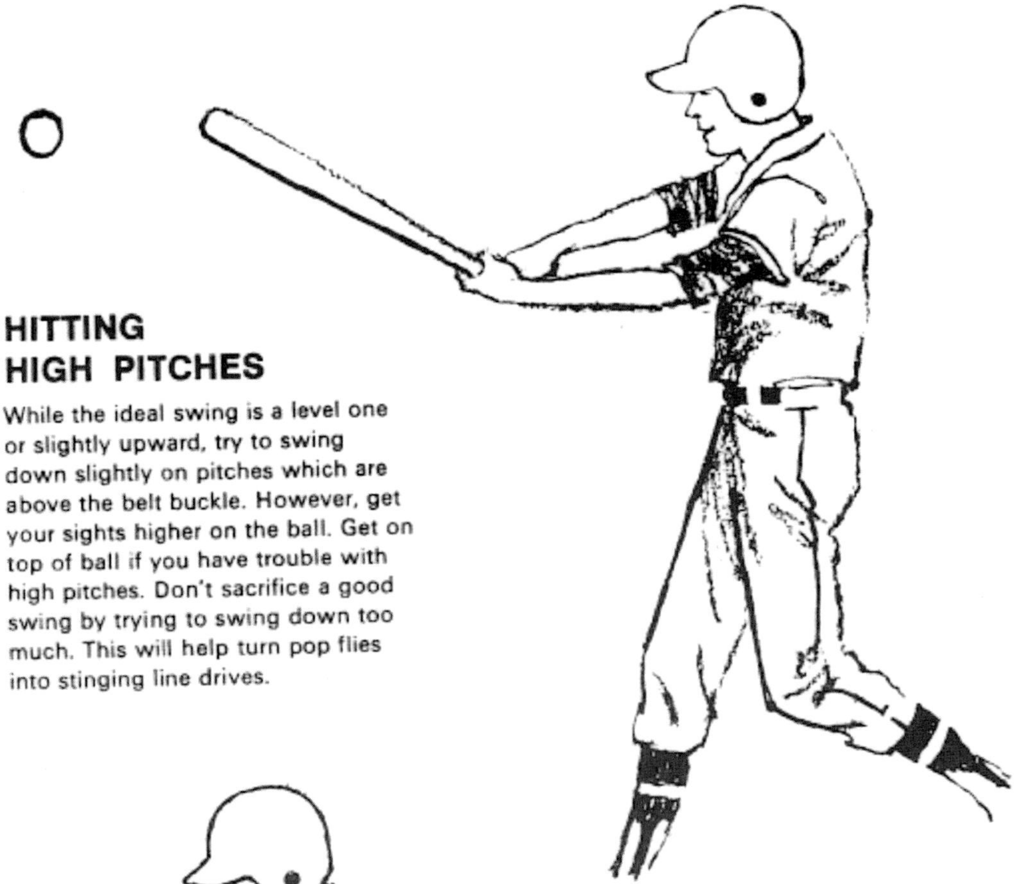

HITTING HIGH PITCHES

While the ideal swing is a level one or slightly upward, try to swing down slightly on pitches which are above the belt buckle. However, get your sights higher on the ball. Get on top of ball if you have trouble with high pitches. Don't sacrifice a good swing by trying to swing down too much. This will help turn pop flies into stinging line drives.

HITTING LOW PITCHES

Swing up slightly on pitches which are below the belt buckle. Think in terms of bending or going down to low balls.

GETTING IN SHAPE IS THE "NAME OF THE GAME"

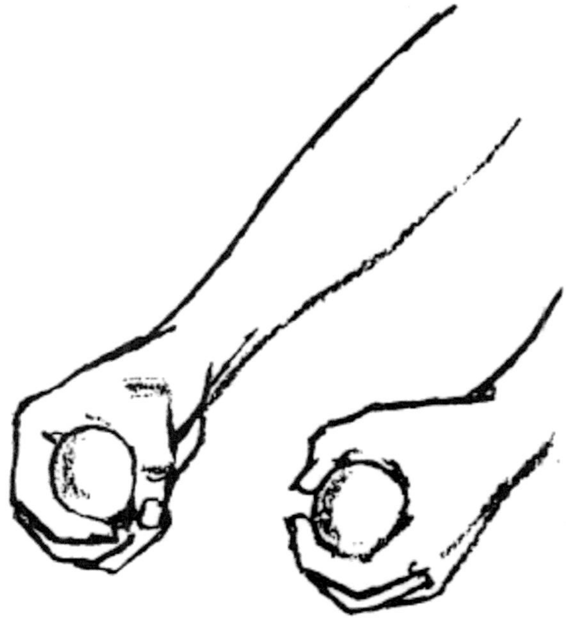

STAY IN GOOD PHYSICAL CONDITION

A systematic physical fitness program is a part of the game of baseball. Get all the rest you need and get it regularly! Eat a well-balanced diet. Develop strong hands by swinging a bat eight or ten ounces heavier than the one you'd usually use in a game or squeezing a rubber ball.

DEVELOP STRONG LEGS

Before you even pick up a bat at the beginning of the season, do some roadwork . . . especially if you are on the heavy side. Tossing a ball, swinging a bat, stretching, jogging are other good ways to get into shape. You might also want to invest in the type of Physical Fitness equipment that you can use to keep in training all year around such as a set of barbells.

DEVELOP A GOOD MENTAL ATTITUDE

The best mental attitude I can think of for a batter is a burning desire to hit the cover off the ball every time he comes up to bat. I don't mean home runs but just good solid base hits. Learn something from every pitch, whether you hit it, miss it or let it go by. Practice constantly and concentrate on your weak points. If you have trouble hitting balls above your waist or below it get someone to throw you these kind of pitches until you learn how to hit them.

HOW TO HANDLE A BATTING SLUMP

A batting slump means only one thing . . . the pitchers are fooling you more often. Stay loose. Don't get discouraged. If you are popping up, get your sights up higher on the ball. If you're not getting enough power maybe you are not putting enough of your hip behind your swing. Don't be afraid to experiment. Learn to hit to the opposite field. Try choking up slightly on your bat or move away from the plate a bit. Either of these actions let you take a longer look at the pitch by delaying the start of your swing.

FIELDING TIPS

Here are some of the basics of fielding I remind my young players of, when they come to spring training. When you are in the outfield make up your mind where you are going to throw the ball if it is hit to you. If there is someone on base throw to the base which gives you the best chance of cutting down the runner.

Playing the infield or the outfield takes a lot of hustle. Be aggressive and move towards ground balls instead of waiting for them to come to you, keeping your glove wide open. Use both hands whenever possible to catch the ball.

With runners on base do everything you can to get your glove on the ball and keep it in the infield. Take time to throw accurately, even if it means missing a double play on occasion. Practice your footwork whenever you can. And here it's even more important to make up your mind what you are going to do with the ball *before* it is hit to you.

One of the most difficult plays for youngsters to learn is tagging out a base runner. If you have the baseline well covered you don't have to worry about trying to chase the runner. Grip the ball firmly and simply let the runner tag himself out.

WHAT TO LOOK FOR IN A FIELDER'S GLOVE

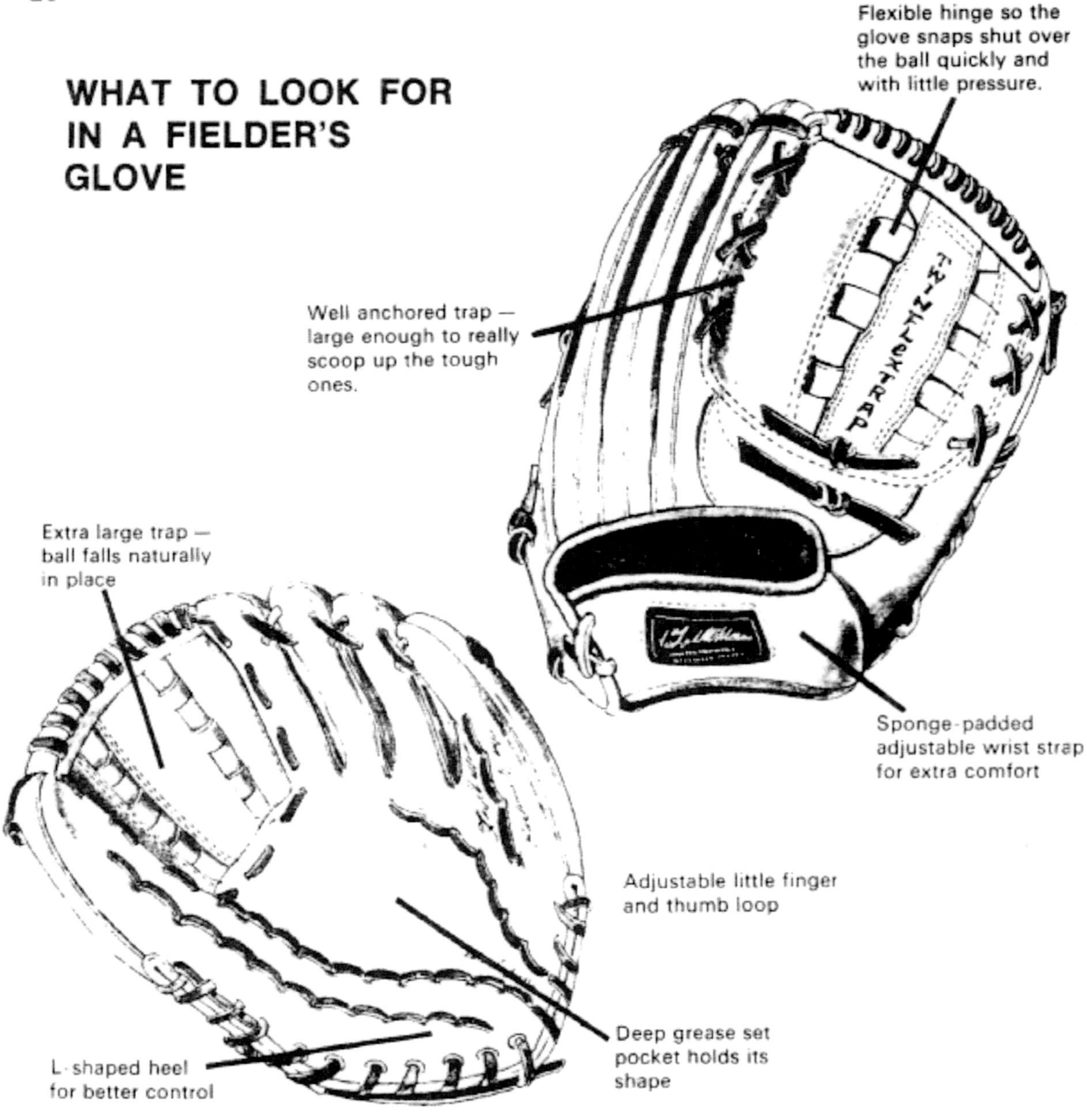

As far as fielder's gloves are concerned, I worked with Sears to design one that suits me and many young players I know to a "T". It has a double-action trap that's so large we put lacing down the finger and thumb to hold it in shape. The Flex-Action hinge makes hanging on to those hot ones a "snap". And this glove is made from U.S. top grain cowhide which will last for many seasons of play. It also has a smooth comfortable lining. This is a professional quality glove . . . and believe me, it doesn't pay to skimp on quality when you are buying a baseball glove.

SELECTING A FIRST BASEMAN'S GLOVE

Since a first baseman uses his glove more than any player besides the catcher it's important to have a good one. Look for features such as a Laced Split Trap, Flex-Action Hinge. Make sure that you have a big pocket for scooping up grounders and hanging on to hot liners.

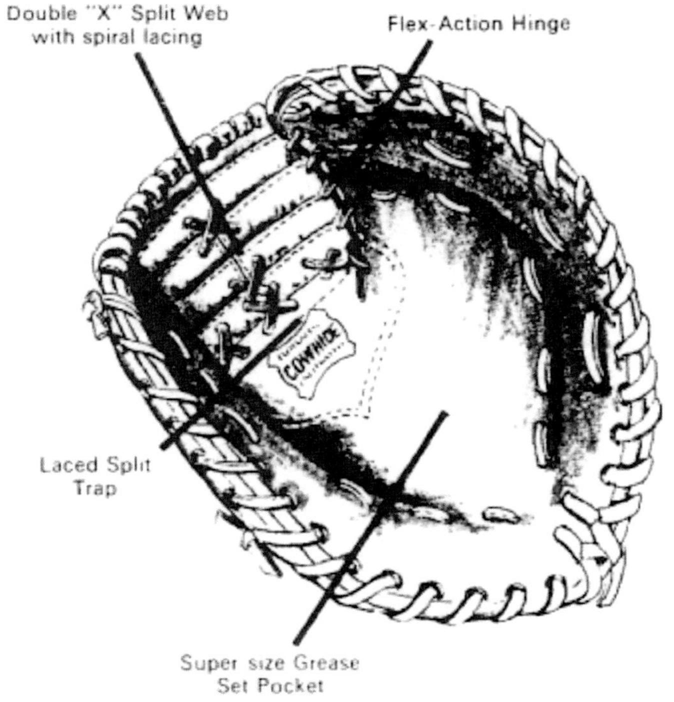

SELECTING A CATCHER'S MITT

When buying a Catcher's mitt check out the type of pocket thoroughly. Many catchers I know prefer the two-piece barrel-shaped type that has a half-center split for extra flexibility. Be sure the pocket is well padded — laminated foam rubber and felt hold their shape for a long, long time.

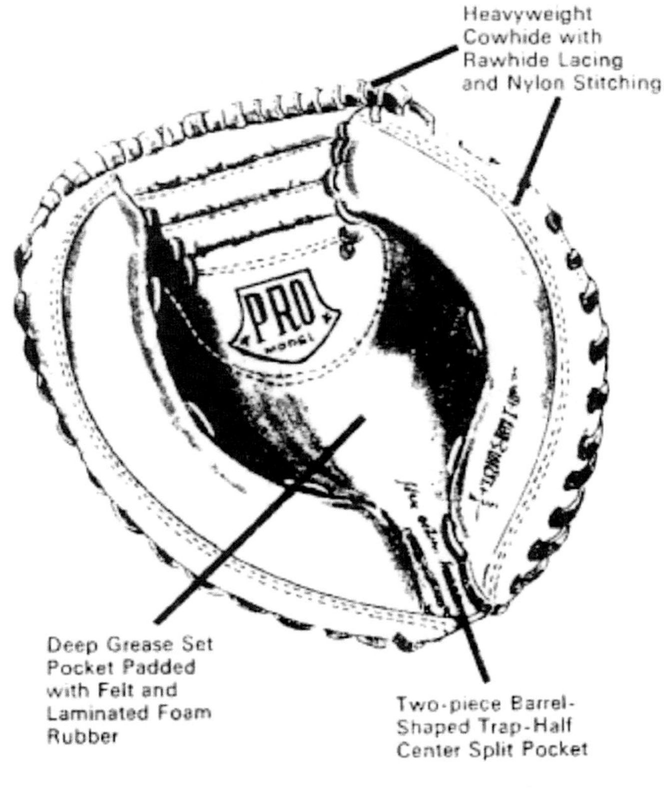

MAKE SURE YOU HAVE PROPER EQUIPMENT

In addition to a good glove, bat, baseball, shoes and uniform there are other items of essential equipment. These include protective equipment such as masks, body protectors and leg guards for catchers and batting helmets for batters. I firmly believe that every player, regardless of position, should get in the habit of wearing a supporter and a cup. In the game of baseball you never know when a ball is going to take a bad hop. A long sleeved cotton sweatshirt is ideal for workouts and for wearing under the uniform during games.

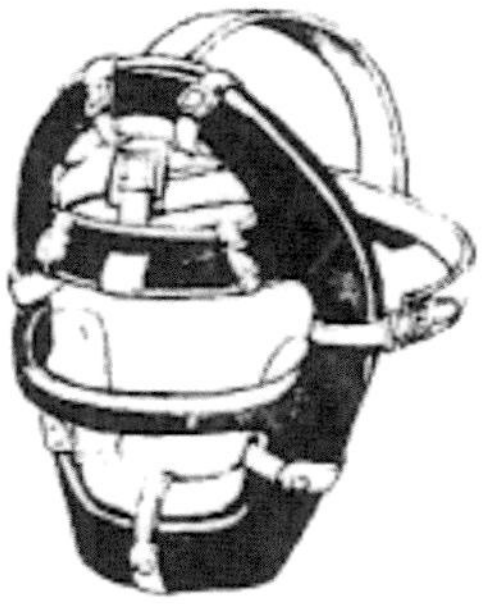

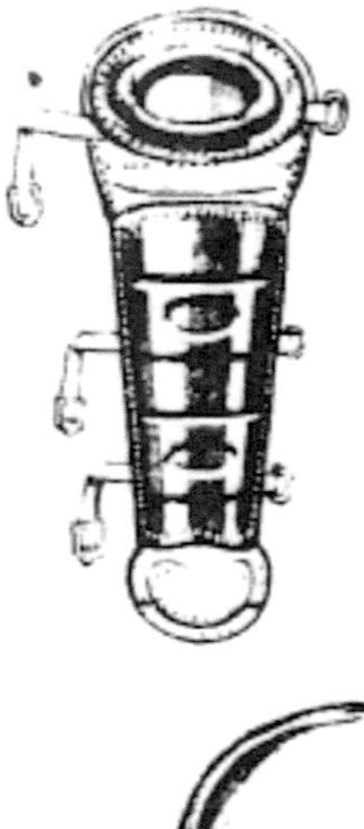

TAKE GOOD CARE OF YOUR EQUIPMENT

Keeping your baseball shoes polished and your glove oiled will make them last longer and perform more satisfactorily. Don't leave gloves or shoes outside where the sun and the rain can get at them. Bats should be stored someplace where it is not too dry or too humid.

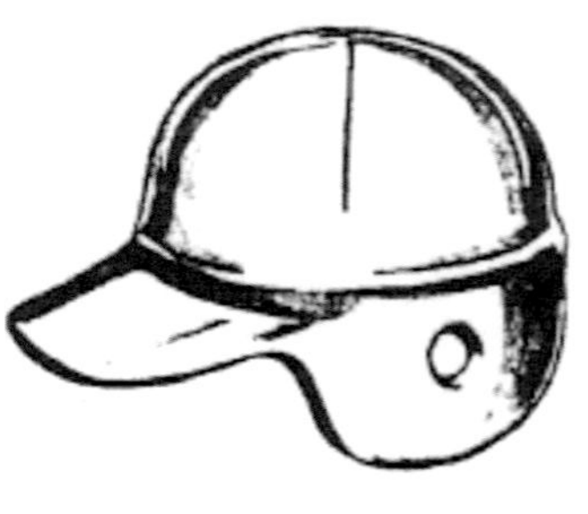

LAKEVILLE

BAEBALL CAMP INC.

Lakeville, Mass 02346

Dear Camper:

It probably doesn't seem very long ago that you were packing your bags to come to camp. Now you have completed your camp stay and it is our hope that is has been a profitable and enjoyable one.

The TED WILLIAMS CAMP has been fortunate in having, for many years, skilled and dedicated men who have made every effort to help you add valuable experiences to you store of knowledge in the game of baseball.

Your coach has submitted the Evaluation Progress Report on the reverse side. It states his opinion of your performance while at camp. The enclosed literature has many helpful suggestions you may want to use to help you improve your game.

The entire TED WILLIAMS CAMP ADMINISTRATION and STAFF join me in wishing you a Great Baseball Summer. WE HAVE ENJOYED HAVING YOU and HOPE TO SEE YOU AGAIN.

Sincerely;

TED WILLIAMS CAMP

(Signed Bernard J. Cassidy)

Bernard J. Cassidy

Executive Director

The following is a copy of a note that was sent to the parents of Campers at the end of the camping season. It had attached "evaluations" of the individual campers' conduct and accomplishments during the previous season. (It was printed on a yellow card.)

THE TED WILLIAMS CAMP has had another successful camping season. Boys are our business and we hope these many evaluations of your boy will be meaningful to you.

We are looking forward to the return of your boy to next year's camping season.

Best for the future.

Art Gillespie
Camp Director

This small card accompanied the reports which were sent to parents at the conclusion of each camp season. Campers were evaluated "in all major camping. areas" by at least six different camp personnel, and were graded on a system from 1 to 5.

Note: The above was obtained from "RECOLLECTING NEMASKET"

"Writing about the history of Middleboro & Lakeville, Massachusetts" Monday, August 17, 2009 Posted by Mike

TED WILLIAMS JUNIOR CAMPER DRESS "T" SHIRT

This, #41 "T" shirt, worn by a 7 year old Camper, #295 (written inside the collar) was found with Ted's souvenirs in the home that he sold in Middleboro, MA in 1975.

Each Camper had a "dress" uniform that was worn when playing a public-attended baseball game at home or away. An every day white "T" shirt with the "TED WILLIAMS CAMP" logo printed on the chest would be worn during practice sessions in the morning and during the afternoon intramural games on one of the 5 Camp ball fields.

The Camp was learning a lot about discipline in the early years.

Camp ended at the end of August. Campers went home to their families to begin their school year. The coaches finalized their report cards for each camper, which were then mailed to their homes. The report included the boys' participation in baseball and graded his ability from the beginning to the end of his session. It stated his deportment, willingness to follow the rules, and growth as a member of a team.

The Partners, including Ted, met to summarize the results of their first year.

Overall, it was very successful. The tuition did not cover the accrued expenses. Ted was happy with the results and continued to commit to "Make it work!" They agreed to increase the attendance from 125 in the following year - 1959. Al, Bernie, and Lester could relax a bit, but their full-time attention would still be required until the Camp opened again in June 1959.

TED SPENT THE FALL FISHING IN CANADA AND WINTER FISHING IN FLORIDA

CHAPTER: 11

CAMP CONTINUES 2ND & 3RD YEAR 1959-1960

The Middleboro Gazette July 2, 1959

> "The Ted Williams Camp in Lakeville opened officially for the summer season Saturday. Baseball coaches for the season at the camp are Roy Engle of San Diego, Cal., Dale Patterson of South Hanen, Mich., "Wos" Caldwell of Gainesville, Fla., and Albert Palmeira of New Bedford; swimming instructor, Richard Setteducati of New Bedford, program director, Henry League of New Bedford; riding instructor Albert Arsenault of Taunton; Miss Harriet Martin, R.N. of New Bedford; Chef, Albert T. Moniz of New Bedford and Sandra Weeks of Taunton; sanitation, James Taylor of New Bedford and salad chef John Moniz of New Bedford."

The 1959 Boys Baseball Camp opened on time after receiving "Live-In" Campers from away a couple of days before the opening day. Orientation classes conducted by Partners Al, Bernie, and Lester made the campers feel welcome. Many were repeat campers from the previous year, which helped to make the new Campers feel more comfortable. The Counselor assigned to the specific quarters assisted in the process.

The local boys who lived at home were also included in the orientation classes. Part of the orientation process included forming the team that they would start out playing with. Team building was an important part of the program.

Again, the town of Lakeville was awakened to the presence of many new faces.

Autos from far away, including some from adjoining States, were bringing their sons to the Camp. Delivery trucks with supplies added to the increased activity. Many of the staff were commuting daily. Only two roads crossed between the Camp and the small business centre. There were no traffic lights. Nobody complained.

The Camp became more of a fixture in the town of Lakeville. The partners were still fine-tuning their operation. They added to and improved the camp facilities. They increased enrollment and the amount they charged for each student at each session. The income was coming close to being self-sustaining financially, with Ted still contributing a few thousand dollars each year into the checking account so that the partners were able to keep up with the bills.

Bernie Cassidy and his wife Terry worked out of the Camp office full-time during the active Camp months and in the off-season. They also maintained cash balances for each of the Campers during the summer while they enjoyed playing baseball.

Ted had two very good years playing for the Red Sox in 1957 and 1958, with batting averages of .388 and .329 and record annual salaries of $125,000 in 1958 and 1959.

Then tragedy struck. Ted suffered a bad crick in his neck during the 1959 spring training. It was diagnosed as a pinched nerve, which required him to be in traction for three weeks. He toughed out the season, but his batting average dropped to .254.

Tom Yawkey, the president of the Red Sox, called Ted into his office at the season's end and asked, "What are you going to do?" This took Ted by surprise; he hesitated and returned with the question, "What do you think I should do?" Yawkey reminded Ted he had only one year left in his contract and suggested, "I think you should retire." This hit Ted by surprise. He hesitated and took his time to think it through without showing any anger. Then said. "Tom, I really think that I will be able to play well next year. I ask you to let me think it through during the winter. I will truthfully evaluate my condition before Spring Training and retire if I do not think I can play up to my full potential. I ask that you reduce my annual contract salary from the current $125,000 by one-third to $90,000. I did not earn my last year's salary."

TED'S INTEGRITY COMES THROUGH - AGAIN

Tom accepted this answer. Ted wondered how he would be able to maintain his standard of living the following year given his commitments of owning property in Canada and Florida, divorce and child support, and the Boys Baseball Camp.

Ted had many investments and active sponsor income, including Wilson Sporting Goods, a fishing tackle manufacturer in CT, and various food and clothing companies. But nothing of lasting or sufficient income for the many years ahead. Then, one day, while fishing with a friend, the friend suggested he contact Sears and Roebuck.

They were a very large multi-distributor of all kinds of goods. The national sporting industry was gaining in popularity, including basketball, football, and baseball. Maybe they would be interested in his services.

During the 1960 baseball season, Ted was in Chicago with the Red Sox and courting his new girlfriend, a beautiful socialite, Lee Howard, who lived there. He contacted Sears at their headquarters and met with their marketing manager, who quickly accepted Ted's offer of a five-year contract for the same $125,000 per year he previously had with the Red Sox. He would head up a new "Sports Advisory Group" and personally be in charge of the baseball, fishing and hunting equipment that Sears sold. The other sports products would have similar advisory managers who would report to Ted. The Advisory Group would meet a few times a year. The advisors would attend special events at selected stores, and Ted would be called upon to appear personally when needed. He had the freedom to effectively be his own boss.

He would evaluate equipment before Sears introduced them, thus assuring that the quality of their product met his standards.

He once was with a Sears executive who referred to a fishing rod as a "Fishing Pole," Ted immediately corrected him by saying, "We only sell Fishing Rods in our business - Poles are for kids catching catfish."

Ted's future was assured. He could continue to conduct his personal activity at his own discretion, including his full support of his Boys Baseball Camp in Lakeville.

Lee Howard was from a wealthy Chicago family and enjoyed the nicest things money could buy. She was very attractive and intelligent. She also had the talent to appear in Hollywood films. She was previously married and was the active parent of two children when she met Ted in 1959. She loved him immediately for his positive manner and being tall and handsome. He splurged on her with expensive gifts and romance. Ted made it known he had a child and had no interest in having more children. She had no interest in having more children either. They were compatible from the beginning.

The Ted Williams Boys Baseball Camp Closed Saturday, August 25th, with their annual last-night get-together around a campfire on the shore of Loon Pond. Director Dale Patterson spoke about the good season they had. Awards were handed out. (No mention of the appearance of Ted Williams? He must have been playing a Red Sox away game.)

Award categories included;

Best Baseball by dorm-- Pitcher, Catcher, Infielder, Outfielder, Hitter, Attitude. 18 awards
Little League All-Stars - Pitcher, Catcher, First Base, Second Base, Short Stop, Third Base,

Left, Center, Right Fielders 9 awards

Pony League All-Stars - ditto above 9 awards

Senior League All-Stars - ditto above 9 awards

All of the above included autographed photos of Ted Williams

Camp All-Stars - ditto above 9 awards

Honor Awards - 2 awards - engraved Loving Cup

Sailing Awards - 4 awards

Special Camp Award - 1 award Autographed Baseball and small bat and photo

Saturday was moving day with a lot of activity, including families picking up their sons and buses leaving for trains, airports, and bus stations. The partners were there to wish good-bys. On Monday they met to review the excellent season. A routine phone call to Ted was made. Planning for the 1961 season included Ted's full-time presence. Where would he stay during the full season?

Lydia Rotch, a wealthy local woman, had a Guest House on her estate that might be available. This was one of their priority concerns.

On September 28th, 1960, Ted played his last game for the Red Sox, it was on a cold rainy day at Fenway Park, with low attendance. On his last time at bat, he hit his last Major League home run late in the game. A fitting conclusion to achieving his goal to be "the greatest hitter ever to live." His ending batting average was .316 for the year and a .344 lifetime average.

He met his promise to Tom Yawkey that he would play to his potential in this final year. He went out without fanfare. Immediately following the game, he called his girlfriend Lee in Chicago to announce that he had hit a home run in his last at-bat. She said, "Great." That was it. He waited for his Cadillac to be brought to him after the fans had left the park and went straight to his apartment at the Somerset Hotel. That evening, he sponsored a party for his "regular" fans to say "Farewell". No celebrities or newspaper writers were invited.

AGAIN, TED AVOIDED NOTORIETY. THEN, HE WENT FISHING IN FLORIDA.

CHAPTER 12

FISHING IN CANADA 1961

Ted's attraction to fishing in Canada began during one of his appearances in the late 1950s at the annual Boston Sportsmans Show. A group of serious Boston area fishermen formed the Miramichi Anglers Association in the early 1950s and built a large private Lodge on the Miramichi River in New Brunswick, Canada, for their (15) members with room for guests and future members. In 1958, a member approached Ted at the show and invited him to be his guest, explaining the challenging sport of fishing for spawning salmon in the rapids of the Miramichi River, a location that Ted had never tried. Ted accepted.

The Lodge is located 30 miles southwest of the St. Lawrence estuary, where salmon return to spawn in the calm backwater pools along the fast-moving rapids. The members were successful businessmen from the Boston area who could spend considerable time during the regulated fishing season in the Province of New Brunswick.

Ted visited the Lodge in the spring of 1959 and loved the experience. He traded stories and jokes with serious fishermen whose profanity was the norm - not the exception. The locals had no knowledge or interest in professional baseball. They knew Ted's reputation, but it didn't enter conversations. The fishing tested his capability.

Province regulations specified that the licensed fisherman was required to be accompanied by an official paid guide at all times when fishing. Roy Curtis, the local guide assigned to Ted, tested Ted's ability and character, as did Ted about Roy's responsibilities. They each passed the others' tests and became long, fast friends.

The next year, in the spring of 1960, Ted was invited back by the Anglers Association, voted in as a member, and was able to retain Roy as his guide. He was nearing the end of his Red Sox career, and this thought was now in his mind. He decided that he wanted to live in this area in his retirement when not spending the hot summers fishing in Florida and wanted to build a lodge of his own on the river bank of the Miramichi River. He requested Roy to search the area for a suitable location he could purchase.

That year, Roy found the correct parcel of land with access to the river from the local road. This ideal lot was in the Town of Gray Rapids. Ted bought it and again asked his trusted guide to have a fishing lodge built upon it. Roy again accepted the responsibility. The Lodge was completed in 1961 and named "White Birch Lodge." Ted retained Roy and his wife Edna to maintain the property and serve all his and guests' needs while he was there. They provided meals, did laundry and anything else that distracted Ted from fishing.

MIRAMICHI ANGLERS ASSOCIATION - Shadow Box of Flies
and a copy of a required Non-Resident Fishing License

Photo of the 17 flies encased in a shadow box - one for each member tied by the doner member H. Weimer Haynes in 1960.

Note: The fly for the SLUGGER Ted Williams appears at the bottom right in the box.

Members Lapel Button

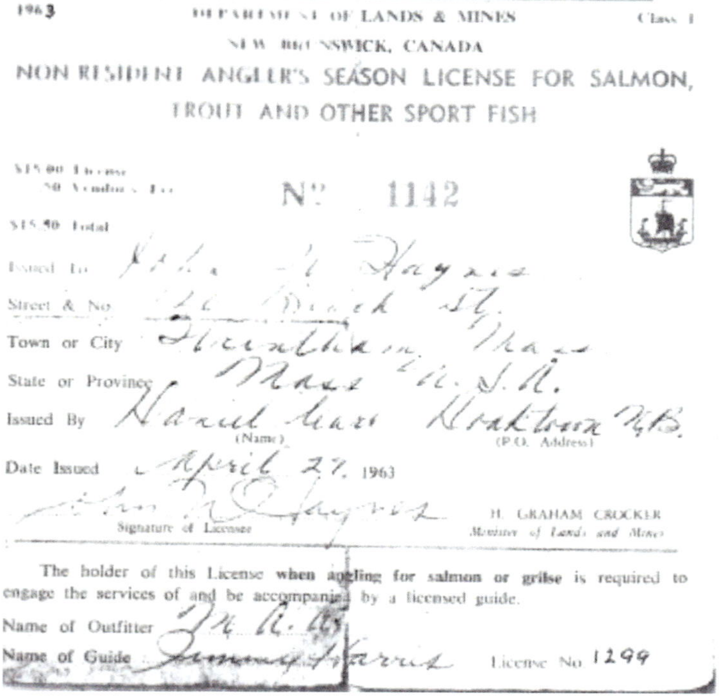

1963 DEPARTMENT OF LANDS & MINES Class 1
NEW BRUNSWICK, CANADA
NON RESIDENT ANGLER'S SEASON LICENSE FOR SALMON, TROUT AND OTHER SPORT FISH

$15.00 License
.50 Vendor's Fee
$15.50 Total

No 1142

Issued To John W. Haynes
Street & No. 26 Birch St.
Town or City Wrentham, Mass.
State or Province Mass. U.S.A.
Issued By Harold [illegible] (Name) Doaktown, N.B. (P.O. Address)
Date Issued April 27, 1963
John W. Haynes
Signature of Licensee
H. GRAHAM CROCKER
Minister of Lands and Mines

The holder of this License when angling for salmon or grilse is required to engage the services of and be accompanied by a licensed guide.
Name of Outfitter [illegible]
Name of Guide Jimmy Harris License No. 1299

April 1963
Fishing License issued to John W. Haynes son of Weimer Haynes

Note: The name of the Fishing Guide Jimmy Harris who was assigned to accompany John at all times when fishing

This property became his most favoured home until he died in 2002. The property has been expanded with the addition of new cottages and continues to be rented today by the current owners to serious fishing parties.

In the meantime, in 1960, H. Weimer Haynes, the new member of the Miramichi Anglers Association, took it upon himself to make (17) shadowboxes, one for each of the current members, which displays the favoured fly of each member including his own - "EXECUTER (Haynes)" located in the upper right corner, and Ted's - "The SLUGGER" (Williams)" in the lower right corner for a total of (289) flies. Ted was proficient in the tying of flies and assisted Weimer in this effort.

The Weimer Haynes shadowbox hangs on the wall today in the home of his son, John Haynes, a good friend and co-worker of mine. (see photo at the end of this chapter)This background story is part of Ted's "Overlooked Legacy" because it highlights his love of the outdoors, mingling with regular people at a time when he was contemplating his future beyond professional baseball and when, in 1957, he committed himself to the creation of a Boys Baseball Camp in Lakeville, MA. Each of his two wives, Lee and Deloris, lived with him both in New Brunswick, Canada and in the Boys Camp in Lakeville.

These two locations, as well as his third home in Islamorada, Florida, were the closest thing to a permanent home Ted had had since childhood. Ted lived most of his baseball career in a hotel in Boston and in other cities where he played ball. He also lived in Navy and Marine barracks during WW II and the Korean War. The trunks of his cars were filled with suitcases and fishing gear.

CHAPTER 13

TED AT CAMP FULL TIME 1961 - 1968

Ted retired from the Red Sox in Sept 1960 and now could concentrate on supervising Camp operations full time during the 8-week summer sessions in 1961.

His three partners with the able assistance of their wives had fine-tuned the first three years of operation. Now in 1961, they were adapting to necessary staff changes, new faces of boys reporting for the first time as well as repeat boy Campers and insuring that all facilities were ready for occupancy. They also were anxious to now have Ted present for the first time on a full-time basis.

The Camp was now financially stable, with income sufficient to pay the current bills. Ted's early contributions were just that. Ted was happy he was able to continue to make the project successful when his gifts of money were needed.

Lester was appointed to be a "Special Policeman, ready for general duty" by the town Selectmen during July's meeting. The partners continued to be active citizens within their community.

Ted arrived in his new 1961 Cadilac convertible, complete with a suitcase, fishing poles, and items necessary to make fishing flies. The big question was where he would stay for his first full season overseeing Camp operations.

The partners anticipated this situation and had made arrangements for Ted to meet a local lady who might be able to answer this dilemma.

The answer came when he was introduced to Lydia Rotch, a single wealthy woman who lived alone on a large estate bordering Long Pond of Highland Road a short distance from the Boys Camp. She lived in a large two-story sprawling house named "Stonehouse" on Apponequet Drive, a private dirt road with a formal stone entrance and with a "Guest House" further up the Drive. Both homes had views of Long Pond and good fishing. Ted and Lydia immediately struck up a friendship. She was the outdoors type, owning many horses and ponies which she rented out and which she allowed patrons to trail the horses on her estate. She owned her own airplane. She was an artist and enjoyed sculpturing. She was athletic and golfed on her own private nine-hole golf course, which surrounded Stonehouse. And she was a serious fan of the Red Sox.

They formed a close relationship. Ted was in his best form with "Hiya Sport" down home manner and was strikingly handsome. How could she not invite him to rent her available Guest House? The deal was done. She subsequently named two of her horses "SLUGGER" and "HOME RUN" after him.

Ted was now available to supervise his Boys Baseball Camp. His immediate action was to make sure that the camp facilities were kept in excellent condition and to ensure the boys were well disciplined in their activities as well as in their free time. This was to be a time of building character and integrity while having fun learning how to play the national sport of baseball. Full attention was paid to keeping things clean and healthy. His demands for a military style of operation were key. He attended reveille at 6 am when the full complement of Campers and Staff were present to raise the US flag and Pledge of Allegiance while the National Anthem played over the loudspeaker system. A roll call was taken. Then, he would visit the dining hall to share his breakfast with the boys and witness breakfast operations.

A loudspeaker system would announce the beginning of the morning training program. The boys knew where to go to get their instruction for, pitching, hitting, catching, runnning the bases, infielding and outfielding and now umpiring. Ted would visit each site and comment with accolades or constructive comments. He made sure that his presence added to the fun of the program. He could be seen riding a bicycle to each of the scattered sites. That in itself would have been interesting because of his six foot three inch body reaching out in all directions. He wore a black uniform while the senior coaches wore White jerseys, the younger counselors wore Yellow jerseys and the boys wore White "T" shirts with the Ted Williams Boys Baseball Camp logo printed on the chest. Their registration number was written inside the collar for easy identification after being laundered.

Following lunch and a brief rest period, the much-awaited actual playing of a ball game on each of the five ball fields was announced. Learning in the morning was enjoyable, but actually playing what was learned made it fun. Following the evening meal there was usually optional entertainment such as movies, swimming, riding horses or even attending an entertaining talk given by one of Teds Red Sox past teammates. Johnny Pesky was often invited. Weekend programs were scheduled, including the best players organized as a team who would play a game at home or away against the best in rival towns. The boys had special dress playing uniforms to wear on these frequent occasions.

Lester Warburton hired 16-year-old Paul Dumas and a friend of his to paint the office, dining hall, dormitory, and other buildings, "Dark Brown," on the campsite grounds. The boys were neighbors of Lester, and they "Hung Out" at the Cassidy-owned Lakeview Drive-In Restaurant, watching the "Cute Car Hop" girls while eating their ice cream cones. The restaurant was also called "Gulf Hill Ice Cream Shop". Lester would drive them the 5 miles to the Camp where he also was working, then bring them home at the end of the work day. Paul said Lester "was a good man". He didn't remember meeting Albert H. Cassidy.

In the spring of 1961, Ted accepted the job as a coach at Red Sox Spring training in Scottsdale, Arizona. He was not all that excited about the job but did enjoy coaching the new exciting player Carl Yastrzemsky with his hitting methods. They became good friends.

PLOT OF LAND OWNED BY LAKEVILLE BASEBALL CAMP, INC.
SOLD TO: ALBERT H. CASSIDY - PRESIDENT OF THE CORPORATION - JANUARY 1964

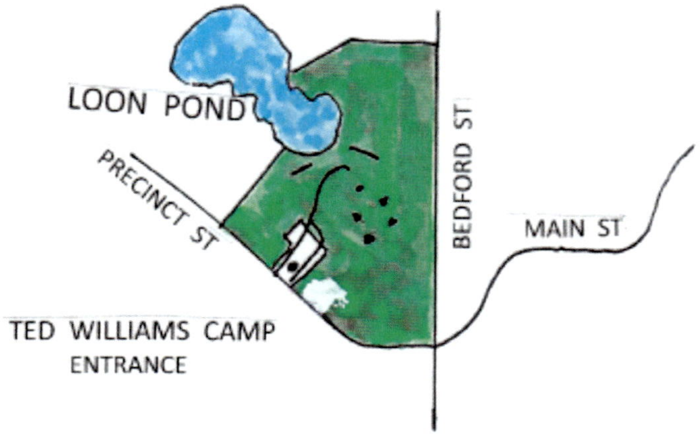

Deed - Book 3085 Pg 450, 451, 452 January 8, 1964

Plot of land owned by LAKEVILLE BASEBALL CAMP, INC. , formally known as Ted Williams Camp Inc., was sold to Albert H. Cassidy, President of the Corporation in January 1964 by vote of shareholders, Ted Williams, AlbertH. Cassidy Bernard Cassidy and Lester Warburton

Note: The diagram is my best attempt to show the size and shape of the property located at the entrance to the Camp Property. It includes a "Right to pass and repass to and from" the Camp property.

The house located on this site was the "Garrish House" previously located on the shore of Loon Pond when the property was owned by the Boston Council of Boy Scouts prior to 1957. The Ted Williams Camp moved it to the entrance of the Camp in 1958. The Camp paid taxes on the entire property prior to this purchase, Albert H. Cassidy began paying $218 taxes on this lot in 1965 and continued to pay taxes thru 1970 when he moved his family to Florida. No taxes were reported paid to the Town of Lakeville on this or the Camp property since then.

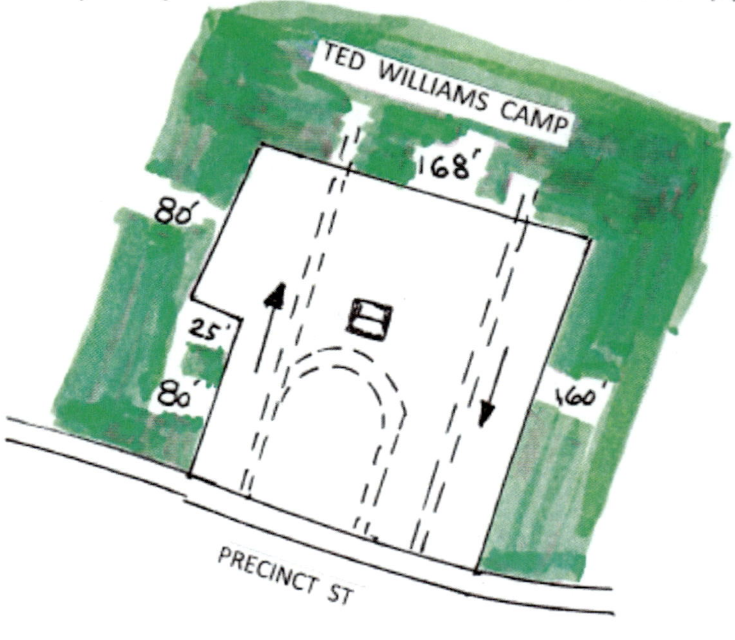

Ted then visited his favored fishing Guide, Roy Curtis, in New Brunswick, Canada, who had found the ideal parcel of land on the Miramichi River in the village of Gray Rapids for Ted to build his fishing lodge. Ted agreed, and the deal was done. He purchased a large piece of land along the shore of the Miramichi River and had Roy take on the job of having Ted's fishing Lodge constructed. Following a few weeks of fly fishing Ted returned to Lakeville and again to review the operations with his partners and inspect the facilities. Ted was a perfectionist.

Ted would receive frequent phone calls in the office and would discard most of the "Return the Call" notes as a waste of time. There was always someone wanting his appearance somewhere to further their own agenda. He would always return a call if it was to help the Dana Faber Cancer Institute and their Jimmy Fund program. He also returned calls to friends and Red Sox ball players looking for assistance in their game. Carl Yastrzemsky was one of these. If Yaz was calling because he was in a batting slump, Ted would call back and discuss Yaz's swing and mental situation, giving helpful instructions. Then, they would stay in touch as a follow-up.

President John F. Kennedy's office in Hyannisport on Cape Cod called and requested that Ted return the call. They wanted Ted to visit the President at his vacation home in Hyannisport. Ted got the message and discarded it. It happened a few days in a row. Al Cassidy was aware of JFK's calls and suggested to Ted that "he had to respond". Ted's answer was, "No, I Don't". Finally, Al asked Ted what he should say if they called again. Ted said, "Tell him I'm a Nixon man!". Ted disliked submitting to the will-not-able people. He preferred being with "regular people."

Ted had other commitments that would take him away on given days. He was now responsible to Sears and Roebuck to fill his Sports Advisory Staff responsibilities. On one such departure, he visited their Chicago Headquarters and mixed business with pleasure by romancing his new girlfriend, Lee Howard.

In 1960, their relationship became very close. They would communicate by letter and make frequent phone calls and visits when possible. Ted was very romantic. He would send flowers and expensive gifts, which she loved receiving. The 1961 Boys Baseball season had come to an end, and Ted visited Sears Headquarters in September. He now had the extra time to spend with Lee.

After a few days with Lee, Ted announced, "We are getting married." "I'll make the arrangements with a friend in the Cambridge, Mass. courthouse to have a justice of the peace marry us, arrange a small party with regular friends and then leave for the Caribbean for our honeymoon." Lee was surprised but didn't hesitate to accept the demand. Not a proposal! She loved Ted and his assertive manner. Ted then went fishing for a few days to his home in the Florida Keys. They both arrived in Cambridge the day before the wedding, Ted from Florida and Lee from Chicago.

On Sept. 16th, 1961, the couple arrived at the courthouse. Ted had his friend John Buckley, the State cop who issued him a warning for speeding in Foxboro, Mass, a few years before and with whom he became a fast friend and a fishing and golfing partner. John served as Best Man and his wife, the Matron of Honor. John was the one who initially introduced Lee to Ted. They had a small party with friends in Lexington and were preparing to leave for Logan Airport when they learned flights to the Caribbean were cancelled due to a hurricane.

Ted had a backup plan. Drive to the Miramichi River in Canada and enjoy their honeymoon fly fishing. The new lodge he had Roy building for him was almost complete. He called ahead and accepted the offer of a local friend whose house was available for them to live while the Lodge was being completed.

Lee and Ted drove the 600 miles, staying overnight halfway in Bangor, ME. They arrived in his Cadillac at midday on September 17th. He went immediately to see his new lodge with Lee. Only minor items were required for occupancy. The next day, he sent Lee to the largest city nearby to purchase furnishings and incidentals while he went back to help complete the lodge. He named it "White Birch Lodge."

Ted outfitted Lee with fly fishing gear and took her out for her first lesson in fly fishing. She did well and tried hard to adjust to this new outdoor sport. Before this, golfing and dining at a local private Chicago golf course was her idea of an outdoor sport.

Lee was introduced to Ted's guide, Roy, and his wife, Edna Curtis, and to a few other fishing friends Ted had made there. Now, she was exposed to the native profane language, not the polite speech to which she was accustomed.

When the furniture arrived, Ted was angry! She had purchased the nicest things money could buy. Ted raised his voice and said, "You are making this a fancy Chicago building suite—not a comfortable fishing lodge. Send it back." She should have taken Edna with her on the buying spree. She did so when she returned the china and silverware and purchased the more acceptable plain dinnerware.

The fishing season officially ended in early October on the Miramichi River. They drove the 1600 miles south to his established home in Islamorada, on the Florida Keys, for the winter and more fishing. Lee again tried to adapt to her new life with Ted, thinking she could "Climb the ladder" of his love for baseball first, fishing second and a wife third.

Ted was more relaxed in Florida and romanced Lee to the best of his ability while still teaching Lee to fish. She did well but did not enjoy it. Ted had a workshop in the back of the house where he would spend hours tying intricate flies. "He'd have me out there and try to teach me. It's difficult. I didn't find it too exciting". Lee took Ted to the local golf club, which she liked best. "That's where he would throw his clubs after hitting a bad shot. He would get profane and show a violent temper. I had him taking calcium pills to help control his temper. They did not have Prozac at that time".

Albert H. Cassidy, the executive director of Ted's baseball camp, was then living on

Precinct St in Lakeville, having moved his family and father from their prior home five miles away. His father was the taxpayer at that time. Al resigned from the Lakeville Industrial and Development Commission on January 11, 1962. Time constraints?

Ted had given up Coaching Red Sox Spring Training. Lee and Ted arrived in Lakeville before the 1962 Boys' Baseball season began and settled in at the Lydia Rotch Guest House. Ted again integrated himself into the community with Lee. He met with his partners and began welcoming the new Campers. This time, more boys repeated their happy experiences than the year before, adding to the overall atmosphere of a successful year to follow.

The partners became active advertising on June 7 in the local Middleboro Gazette newspaper, a new "Girls - Hill Top Camp - Ages 7-17" and the "Ted Williams Boys Camp - Ages 8-17."

"FREE TRANSPORTATION AND A FREE HOT LUNCH" was highlighted.

"Golfing, Archery, Water Skiing, Canoeing, Tennis and Horseback Riding" were offered for both Girls and Boys.

"A Complete Baseball Program and Rifle Range" were added for Boys. "Softball and Crafts" were added for Girls.

The "Girls Hill Top Camp" would occupy Lydia Rotche's Stonehouse for those girls who would now live as full-time Campers.

The advertisement was probably written by Albert H. Cassidy, the Camp's Executive Director, but advertised too early because of his enthusiasm.

On June 15th, Lydia Rotch, the owner of a large estate on Highland Road, two miles from the Boys Camp on Precinct St., filed a petition with the Lakeville Zoning Board of Appeals, seeking a "variance" to permit the use of her estate for an extension to the Boys Camp.

On June 21st a public hearing was held, The board took the request "under advisement, subsequently permitting the use as a camp in a residential district."

Late in July, Robert K. Kroker, a neighbour who lived across the street from Apponoquet Drive, the entrance to the proposed Girls Camp, filed an injunction with the Boston Superior Court to stop the operation of the Camp, which was operating full scale at the time. The complaint cited that the Appeals Board exceeded their authority and that the added traffic congestion and noise violated the law. In August, the judge said, "They are not going to do any more harm by being there for the next two weeks of operation." 250 Lakeville citizens filed a petition indicating that the Camp benefited the town. The case was postponed for further action.

Note: According to a copy of the advertisement "June 23, 1963, to August 24, 1963, Summer Camps—Ted Williams Camp for Boys 8-19, Hill Top Camp for Girls 7-17," it reopened

LAKEVILLE BASEBALL CAMP, INC. (formerly known as Ted Williams Camp, Inc.)

a corporation duly established under the laws of the Commonwealth of Massachusetts and having its usual place of business at Lakeville, Plymouth County, Massachusetts, for consideration paid, grants to ALBERT H. CASSIDY of said Lakeville

with quitclaim covenants

the land, with any buildings thereon, in said Lakeville bounded and described as follows:

File January 8 1964 + Jan 10 1964

The land in Lakeville, Plymouth County, Massachusetts on the northerly side of the Taunton Road known as Precinct Street, also laid out by the County Commissioners by their decree Number 656 and shown on Plan, March 22, 1936, Lewis W. Perkins, County Engineer, bounded and described as follows:

Beginning at a point in the northerly line of said street at an intermediate Plymouth County bound situated 973.885 feet northwest as measured in the line of said street from a Plymouth County bound marking the northwesterly end of a curve shown on said plan having a radius of 980.00 feet in an arc of 636.97 feet; thence

North 29°15' West in line of said street thirty-two (32) feet; thence

North 60°45' East eighty (80) feet; thence

North 29°15' West twenty-five (25) feet; thence

North 60°45' East eighty (80) feet; thence

South 29°15' East one hundred sixty-eight (168) feet; thence

South 60°45' West one hundred sixty (160) feet to the northerly line of said street; thence

In said line north 29°15' West one hundred eleven (111) feet to the bound first mentioned as surveyed by Henry L. Pember, November 1958.

Together with the right to pass and repass to and from said premises and said street over the driveway as now used over an area eighty (80) feet in length and twenty-five (25) feet in width contiguous to and northwesterly from the line hereinbefore described as running North 60°45' East eighty (80) feet from Precinct Street and southwesterly of and contiguous to the line hereinbefore described as North 29°15' West twenty-five (25) feet.

The above described premises are conveyed subject to the real estate taxes assessed thereon for the year 1964 and to all encumbrances of record.

In witness whereof, the said Lakeville Baseball Camp, Inc. has caused its corporate seal to be hereto affixed and these presents to be signed, acknowledged and delivered in its name and behalf by Albert H. Cassidy

its President hereto duly authorized, this 8th day of January in the year one thousand nine hundred and sixty-four.

Signed and sealed in presence of

LAKEVILLE BASEBALL CAMP, INC.

by Albert H. Cassidy
President

on June 23, 1963.

Ted and Lee lived in the Guest house when the Girls' Camp was active. The 9-hole golf course, where the girls and boys played, surrounded the guest house. Ted and Lydia played golf there in the early mornings before Ted left to supervise the Boys at the Camp on Precinct St.

In the summer of 1962, Ted sponsored a dinner for staff and their families in the Loon Pond Dining Hall. Bobby-Jo, Ted's then 13-year-old daughter, visited them and was with them at dinner. One of Ted's disciplines was that you didn't waste food. It was written on the dining hall wall for all scouts to see. Bobby-Jo saw her father get angry, watching many people not finish the food on their plates. Suddenly, he threw his napkin on the floor and said something profane. Bobby-Jo knew someone should pick it up, so she did, maybe suggesting he should calm down.

He spit up a mouthful, which hit her, a pause, and then she ran outside crying. Ted expected discipline from her. People went to her saying her father didn't mean that.

This wasn't the first time she experienced her father's demand for discipline from his children. It lasted and was an issue that continued between her and her father for many years. He also expected this from his wives, and this led to their divorces. He did not apologise for these outbursts but, later in life, acknowledged he had this problem and wished he didn't. Everybody loved Ted and always overlooked this flaw in his personality. He was a Perfectionist. With faults. This was the beginning of the failing marriage between Ted and Lee.

Ted continued to supervise the Camp actively until August 1962, when he and Lee went fishing in Canada and then Florida.

Ted and Lee returned again in June 1963 to supervise the Camp operations.

"Miss Barbra Joyce, the 14-year-old daughter of Ted Williams, was hospitalised at St Luke's hospital in Mibbleboro with a virus while vacationing with her father at the Ted Williams Camp in Lakeville."

Ted met Dolores Wettach on a plane flight back from New Zealand, where he was marketing for Sears Roebuck and where she had had a modelling assignment. He had dinner with her due to connecting flight cancellations from San Francisco. Ted pursued this relationship while still married to Lee and before their divorce on October 13, 1966.

January 8-23, 1964 Deed "The Lakeville Baseball Camp Inc., formally known as Ted Williams Camp, Inc. Grants to Albert H. Cassidy of Lakeville" - a plot of land with a house located at the entrance of the camp on Precinct St. This is the house that had been moved there in 1958 after the Boy Scout property was purchased. Albert H. began paying taxes on this property in 1965. Tax in 1965 was $218. Albert H. and their family moved here from their home on Cassidy Lane, off of County Rd., 5 miles away back in 1962. A vote of the shareholders Ted, Bernie, Albert and Lester approved the sale.

July 9, 1964 "Theodore, "The Kid" Williams will speak at the dedication of Lakeville

Playgrounds Inc. a new baseball diamond at the newly named John Paul Memorial Park on Vaughn St. - Ted will throw out the first pitch in a doubled header as the Tigers meet the Dodgers and the Red Sox meet the Yankees." Ted initiated the unique game of "Blooper Ball" at his Boys Camp in 1961. It did not have an outfield fence to determine a home run. The town added this new field with an outfield fence that would be used for town Little League ball games.

Blooper Ball had many differences from baseball. The ball looked like a softball but larger and softer. The game went fast and for only for six innings. Another big difference was that the pitcher was on the same team as the batter, which created an easy pitch to hit. Its softness assured that a good hit would not clear the fence except when Ted played and routinely hit home runs. This field attracted many fans from surrounding towns, especially when Ted played for his Red Sox team. This was another example of Ted becoming one of the locals and not a celebrity.

TED ENJOYED THE COMPANY OF REGULAR PEOPLE

The 1964 and 1965 Camp years continued to be successful. The partners were working with a slight profit. Ted was still not taking a salary and did not have to contribute finances anymore. Programs were added. The rifle range was closed.

Basketball was now an exciting addition to national sports entertainment, and the local Boston Celtics were leaders. Ted added basketball to the Camp experience by adding a few outdoor courts and extended invitations to Celtics players to speak and demonstrate their talents to very excited Campers when time allowed. Standouts like Dave Cowens and John Havilicek visited. Ted invited other well-known sports pros to assist in seminars on weekends. Johnny Pesky visited many times. These players supported Ted's agenda for excellence, hard work and integrity, building character in those who wanted it while having fun.

Sears Roebuck was still paying Ted $125,000 each year for his active leadership in marketing their products as their Sports Advisory Chairman. He took on the marketing responsibility for baseball, fishing, and hunting equipment. The boating, swimming, and baseball The Rotch Estate areas at the Camp were complete with Sears equipment. The boys had the cash to purchase their own equipment from Steve Stanley's mobile sports store when he visited each week.

Sears was noted for its large catalogues, which were offered free to all customers. They served a double purpose in the Camp "Out Houses" as reading material and toilet paper. The Camp still had many outhouses in the 1960s. Sears renewed Ted's contract for the next five years (1966-1970) at the same salary.

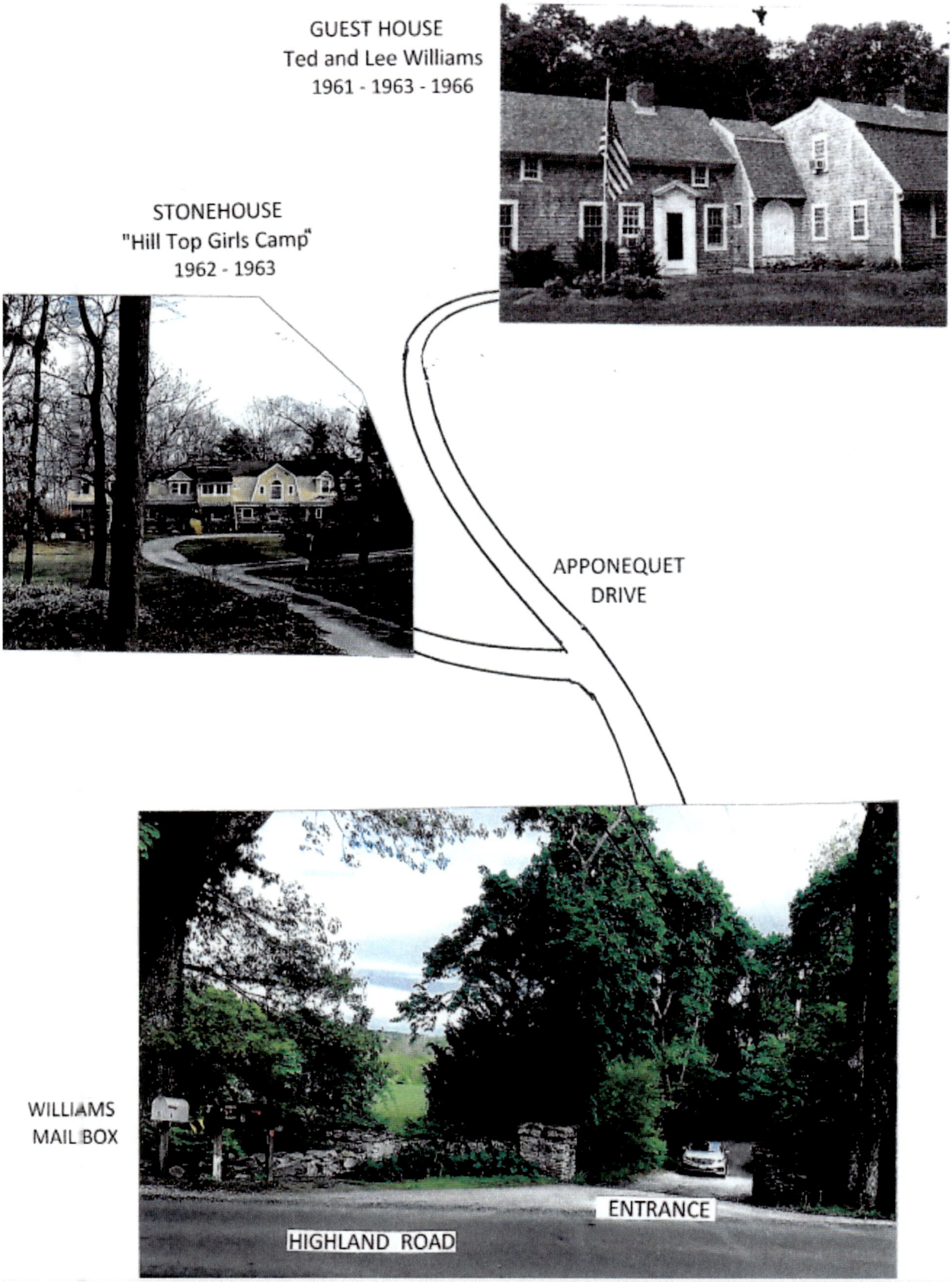
GUEST HOUSE
Ted and Lee Williams
1961 - 1963 - 1966
STONEHOUSE
"Hill Top Girls Camp"
1962 - 1963
APPONEQUET
DRIVE
WILLIAMS
MAIL BOX
ENTRANCE
HIGHLAND ROAD

1966 was another interesting year. The Camp was in good shape except for the day when two Campers, brothers, did not respond at Roll Call one morning. Neither spoke English very well. A frantic search was initiated, including a call to the parents of those who lived in the Montreal, Canada, area. Two days passed when the Camp received a call from the parents that their sons had arrived home safely. They travelled using their thumb the whole way. (How did they avoid Customs at the border?)

The Ted Williams Camp was a summer camp on Loon Pond with baseball as its featured activity, although there were other camp activities such as swimming and fishing. The camp was opened with Ted Williams, No. 9, of the Boston Red Sox, as a partner. It was not uncommon for Williams to make an appearance at the camp to the delight of everyone present. (Courtesy Lakeville Historical Society.)

Note: Gerrish House located at entrance of Ted Williams Camp off of Precinct St. (booklet pg 121)
No entrance yet from Bedford St which was added in 2002

Daylor Consulting Group Inc.	Town Center Aerial Photograph (2001) Lakeville Master Plan	Figure 1

MIDDLEBORO GAZETTE JUNE 7, 1962

ALBERT H CASSIDY
TED WILLIAMS CAMP

Eighteen-year-old daughter Bobby-Jo was married and pregnant. She and her husband eloped and waited weeks before telling her father. She feared that and was close to taking her own life. Ted accepted the situation and found a hospital where she could obtain a lawful abortion. Ted continued to finance his daughter and her husband, but they drifted apart. She had a love-hate relationship with her father, and he with her. She became a distant relative of whom he would not speak for years.

Orville K. Gerrish home on Loon Pond
Images of America booklet by Gail Terry - published 2007 - Pg 117

According to Darryl Bernier April 18, 2024 (see document) the Garrish House was moved from Loon Pond to the current entrance of Ted Williams camp on Precinct St. The town had the Fire Dept burn it down in 2005 and a sign added in 2008 Ted and Les Warburton would stay (rent?) this house when Ted returned to visit between 1970-1986.

The home of Orville K. Gerrish was built about 1889. It was located on Loon Pond and later moved to Precinct Street. In the early 1920s, it was sold to the Boston Council of Boy Scouts for a summer camp. The Ted Williams Camp was located here after the Boston Council of Boy Scouts sold the property. (Courtesy Lakeville Historical Society.)

On January 20, 1966, Ted was invited to the press room at Fenway Park, where they announced he had been elected to the Hall of Fame on the first round of balloting - a record gaining 93% of the votes - another record. He said, "This completes everything a ball player dreams could happen " Then he thanked the writers, saying, "A majority of the press was always with me, only a few against me. If anything, their criticism helped; it spurred me on."

Ted was inducted into the Cooperstown, NY, Baseball Hall of Fame on Monday, July 25, 1966. He left his full-time presence at his Boy's Camp a couple of days early to prepare for the occasion and his acceptance speech. He was nervous. Twenty friends and his pregnant daughter Bobby-Jo were with him. He drew the largest crowd that had ever attended this event. He spoke with his typical humour when he said, "I received two hundred and eighty-odd votes from the writers. I know I don't have two hundred and eighty-odd close friends among the writers." "I want to thank the extras for their vote, thinking I earned it." "The six-minute speech, which Williams read from the handwritten text he'd composed on the Oneonta Hotel stationery, had been delivered flawlessly, with grace, humility, poise, and humour."

Ted had the ability and intelligence to perform when called upon. He did not have a formal education beyond high school. He excelled. He was a perfectionist.

MIDDLEBORO GAZETTE JULY 11, 2002

ADVERTISEMENT OF TED WSILLIAMS SUMMER CAMPS

JUNE 23 1963 TO AUGUST 24 1963

TED WILLIAMS CAMP FOR BOYS 8-19

HILL TOP CAMP - FOR GIRLS 7-17

Then he added to his speech, "I hope someday the names of Satchel Page and Josh Gibson in some way can be added as a symbol of the Negro players that are not here only because they were not given a chance." Ted had always supported the equality of players regardless of their heritage. The Red Sox was the last American League team to hire a Negro, Pumpsie Green. Ten years too late. This statement had slow but significant repercussions. Ted was always outspoken and honestly expressed what was on his mind, but he followed his heart when he had a chance to support someone because of sickness or race. Later in life, according to Al Cassidy Jr., the executor of Ted's estate and son of Albert H. Cassidy, the original partner of Ted's Boys Baseball Camp, said he was present when his father asked Ted "why he had not done more to help the Black cause."

Ted responded, "You're right, but back then, I didn't think I had any authority with Mr. Yawkey". Cassidy Jr suggested that this subject embarrassed him for a long time, and he took this occasion to take a stand on racial equality.

In 1985, a wooden sculpture of Ted was dedicated in the Hall of Fame lobby next to that of Babe Ruth. Ted cried.

TED HAD INTEGRITY

Now living alone, Ted moved from the guest house he rented from Lydia Rotch in the summer of 1966 to a small cabin on Cedardale Rd on the opposite side of Long Pond. He was very involved with Delores Wattach and thought of marrying her. She told Ted she had been a nurse, model, and actress, had had a daughter by a hometown boyfriend that she was never serious about, and had given her daughter up for adoption. They fought a lot; both asserted their independence.

On October 13, 1966, Ted was formally divorced from Lee Howard. This was his second divorce, defined by mental cruelty. 1967 was another eventful year for the now-single Ted Williams. The camp opened on June 25th for its 10th successful year. The waterfront added a Senior Lifesaving course headed by the new "White Shirt" staff member Larry Ewing. Junior Counselors worked to keep the facilities clean and safe. "Safety is the byword at the Ted Williams Camp."

Parmenter Heating Plumbing & Heating Co. completed a year-round plumbing and heating system at the Camp on Precinct St. Is this the end of out houses?

Ted had thoughts of permanently settling down in the Lakeville area. He purchased a house located privately in the middle of a large estate at 361 Marion Rd in Middleboro, MA. It had access to a private fishing spot on Pocksha Pond. The deed was recorded on Sept. 21, 1967, with Ted being stated as being "Unmarried". Friends moved his personal belongings, including boxes and trunks filled with Camp memorabilia, from Cedardale Rd to a locked room on the second floor. He was dating Deloris seriously at this time. "I was smitten with him; he was easy to love," "In the spring of 1968, Deloris told Ted she was pregnant with his child. Williams was incredulous (He could not believe it). He asked if she was sure he was the father.

She said she was quite sure, But Ted wasn't. She said she was hoping he'd propose for three years. You like me, or you don't. That's it!" It took Ted a while to think it through, and he finally decided he should marry her. They were married unceremoniously on their elopement to Kingston, Jamaica, on May 7, 1968. They planned to live in Middleboro during the summers while he supervised his camp.

When interviewed years later, Delores said, "In the summer, we lived in Lakeville. We bought a home there and fixed that up. When fall came, we went to New Brunswick, Canada, and salmon fished till the frost set in. Then we moved down to my farm in Vermont for Christmas and until snow set in, then back to Florida". -The interviewer asked - "Where did you finally locate?"- "We're not located anywhere." "He never located anywhere - He's split up in four separate places. The Keys, Lakeville, Vermont and New Brunswick, Canada."

June 16, 1968, was the opening day of the summer Boys Baseball Camp. "Co-owners of the Camp are Ted Williams, Islamorada, FL; Albert H. Cassidy, Bernard Cassidy and Lester Warburton, all of Lakeville. Albert Palmieri of New Bedford will be the Camp Director. Joseph G. Camacho of Fairhaven will be the Program and Baseball Director.

Their son John Henry was born August 26, 1968, in Burlington, Ton, VT, while Ted lived in his house in Middleboro and attended the final days of the season at his Boys Camp in Lakeville. This was when awards were handed out to Campers before they went home at the end of their camping experience for the year 1968.

In the fall of 1968, Ted received a phone call from the new owner of the lowly Washington Senators baseball team. Bob Short, a wealthy entrepreneur, needed a manager desperately. Ted was comfortable living and fishing at his Islamorada home in the Florida Keys with his uneasy wife Deloris and newborn son John Henry. Bob convinced Ted to meet with him. Ted had an appointment with Sears in Atlanta, and they met there. Ted had no interest in becoming the manager of a major league baseball team. He knew his limitations, and managing was one of them. Then there was his past poor relationship with the press.

However, Ted began to feel he needed additional income now that his second contract with Sears would end the following year. Short offered Ted all kinds of financial and free benefits, which attracted Ted's attention. But he said "No." Short would not stop his active goal to hire Ted. He contacted Joe Cronin, who thought Ted would be a good manager. Joe told Ted that. Short contacted Tom Yawkey, who agreed that Ted would be an asset to the National Baseball League. Ted held firm for a few months, arguing with himself why he should not take the offer - then changing his mind that maybe it would be a good change for him. Deloris was supportive, saying she thought Ted was getting bored and needed a new challenge. Ted himself agreed that he was getting bored.

Ted signed on with the Senators on February 21, 1969, in Bob Shorts' suite at the Washington, D.C. Hilton Hotel.

Thus, Ted would no longer live in his Middleboro, MA home or attend His Boys Camp full time. Ted's partners, Al, Bernie Cassidy, and Lester Warburton would have to continue running the camp without his on-site supervision.

Ted rented his house in Middleboro to Dennis and Joyce Gillette, the good friends of Fred and Margret Corriea, before he and his family, Deloris and baby John Henry, left for Washington. The Gillette's offered to purchase the house, but Ted was not ready to sell. Maybe he thought he would be back if his new job with the Senators didn't work out.

TWO LITTLE LEAGUE BASEBALL BATS AND A BLOOPER BALL
FROM THE TED WILLIAMS BOYS BASEBALL CAMP - 1964

The two well used Baseball Bats and Blooper Ball pictured here were found with other Ted Williams souvenirs in a sealed bedroom after he sold his Middleboro house in 1975.

The very worn, wooden (ash ?) bats are stamped;

TOP BAT: Black Printing

Knob End (Size)	Lower End of Barrel		Upper End of Barrel
2 (32")	BASEBALL EQUIPMENT 1725 Ted Williams (sig.) TM SEARS ROEBUCK AND CO	HOLDFAST -TREATED	APPROVED Ted Williams (sig.) Little League

BOTTOM BAT: Red Printing

Knob End (Size)	Lower End of Barrel		Upper End of Barrel
1 (30 1/2")	BASEBALL EQUIPMENT 1725 240 Ted Williams (sig.) TM SEARS ROEBUCK AND CO	HOLDFAST -TREATED	APPROVED Ted Williams (sig.) Little League

BLOOPER BALL (Compared in size with a regulation baseball)
4 1/2" Dia - Warped - No Markings - White Leather (old age cracking)
Hardened with age - originally very soft

SEP 1 1967 at 10:40 **114531**

RECEIVED BY
CHECKED BY
ABSTRACTED BY Sylva

Statute Form of

Quitclaim Deed

John Cayton, Jr. et ux

TO

Theodore S. Williams

Pd 7 -

7 -

TRANSFER CERTIFICATE OF TITLE ISSUED AND TRANSCRIBED INTO REGISTRATION BOOK 204 PAGE 70 BEING CERTIFICATE NO. 40870 IN PLYMOUTH REGISTRY DISTRICT.

_______________ 19___

at _____ o'clock and _____ minutes _____ m.

Received and Entered with _______________

_______________ Deeds

Book _____ Page _____

Attest:

____
Register

Plymouth Registry District
SEP 1 - 1967

RECEIVED FOR REGISTRATION
10 O'CLOCK 40 m AM

From the Office of

cert

Paul R. Callan, Esq.

Middleboro, Mass.

THE BLAKE PRESS, INC. - PUBLISHERS
BOSTON, MASS.
FORM 152-B

Cert #40870

SEP 3 1975 165833

DATED August . . . . . A.D. 1975.

BETWEEN:

THEODORE S. WILLIAMS,
GRANTOR,

AND:

DENNIS L. GILLETTE ET UX,
GRANTEES

TRANSFER CERTIFICATE OF TITLE ISSUED AND TRANSCRIBED INTO REGISTRATION BOOK 275 PAGE 136 BEING CERTIFICATE NO. 55136 IN PLYMOUTH REGISTRY DISTRICT.

D E E D

SMITH & SMITH
Barristers & Solicitors
P. O. Box 100
Newcastle, N.B.
Canada E1V 3M2

Plymouth Registry District
SEP 3 1975
RECEIVED FOR REGISTRATION
9 O'CLOCK 35 m AM

Sept 3, 1975

Ted Williams to Dennist Joyce Gillette House 361 Marion Road Middleboro, MA

Existing March 2024 dud copy

TED WAS COVERING HIS BASESHIS LEGACY WAS SECURED, YET IT CONTINUED

CHAPTER 14

MEMORIES OF LOCALS 1961 - 1986

The "Overlooked Legacy of Ted Williams" is best understood when talking to todays local residents who have first person recollections of the days when Ted was living full time in Lakeville during the summers of 1961 through 1968.

Each of the following stories is a thread that makes up the fabric of The Legacy, which is a living experience not since told.

It all began with my barber, Fred Correia, telling me of his experience while giving Ted a haircut in 1961. Ted was in his second year of living in Lakeville, and he enjoyed being a regular wherever he went in town. Ted saw that Fred had a fly-casting rod leaning in the corner of his shop and asked Fred about it. Fred said he was teaching himself how to fly cast. Ted, a fly-casting professional, had Fred out in the parking lot, giving him a lesson following the haircut.

Ted and Fred became good friends. It wasn't long after that first fly-casting lesson that Ted asked Fred if he was a good driver. Would he help him drive to New Brunswick, Canada, for a fishing vacation at his new Lodge on the Miramichi River? Fred declined because he had recently married and had not yet had his honeymoon. Fred also had integrity.

On another day, while Fred was cutting Ted's hair, Fred noticed a friend outside his shop and asked Ted if he would speak to him because his friend had just lost his wife to cancer. His friend was a Ted Williams and Red Sox fan. When the friend came into the shop, Ted treated him like one of his old pals and showed him compassion, taking the time to help the man through a difficult time.

Fred said, "Writers expected Ted to kneel at his feet. He wasn't like that. People said he was opinionated, but that was because he knew what he was talking about. He could talk transmissions, baseball, and fly fishing. He was an expert on a lot of subjects."

Fred was also friendly with the Gillettes, who rented the house Ted bought in Middleboro in 1967 and sold in 1975. A Middleboro Gazette newspaper article tells that story.

Gazette Article:

"Dennis Gillette began renting the carriage house on the Morgan estate from Mr. Williams in 1969 and bought the house furnished five years later. I still sleep in his bed, Mr Gillette said, describing the extra-long bookcase bed with the assistance of his wife, Joyce. The carriage house, well off the road with access to Pocksha Pond, was a retreat for the baseball star, who kept his old uniforms and equipment at the house, along with a collection of framed photos, for many years. He changed his mind about selling us the house, but I finally wrote to him, and he conceded."

Richard "Dick" Fickert served on the Board of Selectmen, Board of Health and Lakeville Park Dept, which negotiated the Purchase of Ted Williams Camp for the town in 1986. He said, "We'd sit there by the hour and listen to him tell stories...... Although his Lakeville friends were impressed, people wouldn't generally bother him. Everybody pretty much accepted him as part of the community." Middleboro Gazette August 24, 1963, Will Corey, my VA contact whose office was in the Council on Aging building currently located on the Ted Williams Camp property, he said he pumped gas into Ted's Cadillac Convertable as a ten-year-old at his father's Nash Rambler dealership in Middleboro.

Mary Standish served Ted at the "My Wife and I" convenience store. I was having breakfast at the Nellie Rose breakfast restaurant in Middleboro one Friday morning and asked four departing customers if they had any knowledge of the Ted Williams Camp. Mary stopped and said she did. As a teenager, she made coffee frappes and double cheeseburgers for Ted many noon times from 1961 to 1964 at the "My WIFE and I" convenience store located on Main St near the Camp. The store had a self-serve gasoline pump, sold groceries and had a Soda Fountain with a few tables and chairs where Ted would sit with other locals discussing local gossip while eating his lunch. The Nellie Rose building used to be called "Farrar's Waiting Room" because of its location next to the train station. They made their own ice cream there, and Ted was also a regular customer. He ate a lot of ice cream.

Bruce Baptist, a teenager living in Middleboro in the 1960s, told me at a Friday morning COA Cafe hour that he had friends from church who were Campers. He showed me a pamphlet, "Baseball Basics" by Ted Williams, that was given to him, and copies were given to every Camper when they attended Camp. Later, he worked as a salesperson at a local furniture store and sold Ted a colour TV. Colour TV was very new and expensive in the mid-1960s. A few were being installed locally. Ted bought one, which he may have had installed at the Guest House where he lived.

I met Chris while walking his dog at Ted Williams Park. His wife was a local, and she told him that her brother saw Ted shopping with his daughter Bobby-Jo a few times in 1962 at Mello's grocery store. The store exists today as Starr Market on Main St, a short distance from Fred's barber shop.

Doug Berry was born in Lakeville and was a day camper for the first two years of the Camps existence in 1958 and 1959. He lived on Main St near the Camp and could ride his bicycle through the woods into the park to attend the baseball program with the other 125 boys from around the country. This was when Ted was still playing for the Red Sox and before he was full-time at the Camp. Later, in 1967, Doug attended the Camp for a four-week session at no charge because he would work the other four weeks of the season in the dining room without pay. He and three other locals, Known as "Gally Rats" because they worked in the Camp kitchen, played on the same team that went undefeated for four weeks with a record of 18 wins and O losses. They were the only team to have done that. Ted presented each of them with a Sears and Roebuck bat with his name printed. Doug gave me the bat pictured in this book.

There were approximately 10 teams with 12 or 13 Campers on each team, and they played every afternoon following morning training sessions dedicated to specific facets of the game. Doug played catcher. "Many full-time campers came from across the country and even from foreign countries. Some didn't speak English and were helped by counsellors who could interpret. They were excellent athletes. It was FUN!"

Doug played "Blooper Ball" with Ted. Doug's father fished with Ted on Pocksha Pond, where Ted purchased a house in 1967. His father and uncle would sit with Ted at My Wife and I convenience store and tell fishing stories..

Doug became director of the Camp property after the town of Lakeville purchased it in 1986, ensuring its continued maintenance. He went on to teach and coach sports at the local Apponequet Regional Technical High School, where he is active today.

Doug was woven into the fabric of the town with Ted and enjoyed Ted's meaningful participation with the local "regular" people during the 1960's.

Nancy Johnson LaFave became Ted's personal secretary during the summer of 1966. She had just finished her Junior year of High School taking secretarial courses, and this was her paid summer job. Her father was the fire chief and was aware of Ted's outgoing persona, fearful that his daughter would be exposed to language and acts by Ted that would be disruptive. His negative persona, which was published in Boston's newspapers, was known, but he did not display any negative acts while directing the camp's operation. Nancy said he was active full-time at the Camp that year except when he went to be inducted into the Baseball Hall of Fame. The Office building was located across from the Camp dining hall. She told me, "He was always a perfect gentleman in her presence." He did not swear.

Nancy is now secretary of both the Lakeville Historical Society and Commission and has a great knowledge of the town's history. She told me that Lydia Rotch named two of her horses "Slugger and Home Run." Ted, Lydia, and the three partners arranged to use the Rotch "Stonehouse" as an extension to the Boys and Girls Camp in 1962 and 1963.

Peter Chiuppi ("QP") is an original local and active worker for the Lakeville COA. He received a box of memorabilia that was offered to the public after the town purchased the Camp property in 1986. Many copies of "Baseball Basics" and a red junior "T" shirt were in it. # 295. This box came from the locked 2nd-floor bedroom of the house Ted purchased in Middleboro in 1967 and sold to the Gillettes in 1975. When the real estate broker unlocked the door, they discovered Ted's collection of Camp related items.

Peter met Ted as a child when dining one Sunday in 1965 at the local Golden Spur Restaurant. His father told him to ask Ted for his autograph. He did but has lost it.

Peter also gave me a copy of the July 22, 2002, Boston Globe Pull-Out section D7-14, published 17 days after Ted died. Two memories of Ted's Lakeville Boys Baseball Camp were noted. "Teaching the Masses" article by Greg Perrone, who was an 11-year-old Camper, and "Beating Ted's Team" by Kevin Flanagan of Salem, NH, whose 1979 American Legion team went to Lakeville for the game and won. Note: this was Ten years after Ted left Lakeville to manage the Washington Senators, Ted and his partners were still operating the Boys Camp.

Recently, QP received a thank-you letter from the Cooperstown Baseball Hall of Fame for the copy of "Baseball Basics" they received from an undisclosed person who sent it to them.

Margaret Peg Gross, another local, told me at the COA that her father used to talk with Ted when shopping at Mello's grocery store. She was a classmate of Fred Correia and his wife in high school. More threads of the fabric of Ted Legacy. Wendy Washburn is a volunteer at the Middleboro COA, whom I met while asking strangers if they knew Ted Williams Boys Camp.

Her mother, Helen, played cards with a group that included Katheran Stanley, the wife of Steve Stanley and the owner of Steve's Sports Den on Main St. in Middleboro. Steve provided baseball and other sports equipment and maintained the concession stand at Teds Boys Camp. He was close to Ted. Ted would take dinner at Steve's home, and they would retire to private quarters to talk openly away from the gossipy women., "The Camp boys would line up to purchase things from Steve's truck when he was making deliveries." Many boys were from wealthy families and had the cash to make special purchases."

Rachel Collins and her mother, current owners of the "Guest House" where Ted and Lee lived in the 1960s, showed me a book that was found when they moved into the house. It was written by the original owner, Lydia Rotch, and included a large fold-out map, hand drawn by Lydia, which detailed her estate, including the 9-hole golf course surrounding the Guest House and her Hill Top Farm on Highland Rd. Another item they found was a book which included a CD in a sleeve glued inside the cover. Her mother gave me the CD with the sleeve, which I have played many times. It is a long interview of Ted Williams by his friend and author John Underwood, who wrote the book about his interviews with Ted, "My Turn at Bat".

Roan Barber met Ted at the Boston Sportsman Show when he was a teenager living in Boston. Ted approached him, a custom of Ted's, and asked Roan a few personal questions. He was happy that Roan was interested in Ted's demonstrations. By coincidence, his father, a manager for the Raytheon Co, was transferred to the Lakeville area and bought the Stonehouse from Lydia Rotch's father in 1969 when Roan was 17 years old. Roan went to college to study farming. He returned home, and Lydia Rotch hired him to be the manager of her estate, which he did for 31 years. A friend of Roan's, Joan Gladu Morton, was the manager of Lydia's horse barn for 20 years at the same time. Together, they cared for Lydia, who died in 2002 after being released from the hospital with an incurable illness.

Joan Gladu Morton, now Vice-Chairman of the Lakeville Historical Society and former manager for 20 years of the Lydia Rotch Horse Barn, and her friend Roan Barber never met Ted but have stories of his history while living on the Rotch estate.

Neil Ingraham had coffee with Ted at the "My Wife and I" convenience store in 1965. "He was a nice guy."

Dave Gomes, a 1952 graduate of the Oliver Ames High School, North Easton, MA and a classmate of mine, was active in school sports and a fan of Ted since 1942. He attended Ted's last game at Fenway Park in 1960. Dave was a Marine Honor Guard stationed at Annapolis, MD Military Academy when he and a couple of other Marines in Uniform went to see Ted play for the Red Sox in Baltimore. Ted carried on a conversation with these Marines during the warm-up before the game. He had a chance to meet again with Ted in 1986 at the Marriott Hotel in Anaheim, CA. Ted agreed to have a drink with another Marine veteran but admirers swarmed Ted. It didn't happen but it was agreed upon. Ted was Daves "Hero"

David Heritage, a salesman for a medical company, directed me to a remote department at the Beth Isreal Deaconess Hospital in Plymouth, MA. Again I asked this stranger "if he had any knowledge of the Ted Williams Boys Baseball Camp in Lakeville?" He was surprised at the question coming out of nowhere. He attended the Eaglebrook School for Boys, ages 12-16, in Deerfield, MA, with John Henry, Ted's son, in 1982-83. Ted would visit his son and take him to his Camp at the end of the school year so he could become a Camper for a few weeks while Ted joined his partners in the supervision of the Camp. The Legacy carries on!

Anne Higgins, a member of both the Middleboro and Lakeville Historical Society, was a Junior counsellor in 1958 at the Boys Baseball Camp, which also maintained a "For Pay" Girls Day Camp on Loon Pond. She is the only one to report being disappointed with the camp's management. She and four other young local girlfriends volunteered to work the entire summer as counsellors free of charge.

They taught girls to swim and row boats and follow the required safety rules while at camp. Wilford Booten was the Camp Counselor and their supervisor. He was also responsible for Campers riding horses as part of the Camp experience. She and her friends brought their own lunches. They did not eat lunch in the dining hall with the Camps boys. Her disappointment was because she and her friends never received a "Thank You" for their service. (Note: This oversight is completely against the rules set forth by the partners. They worked hard to gain favour with their neighbours and shared free attendance for work at the Camp. The oversight may have been lost in the major activity required in their first year of operation. I hope and want to believe this.)

Virginia Murdoch was told by a friend, Evelyn Norris, a young woman working at the town Hall, that Ted asked her out for a date. She refused the offer and told her mother of the incident when she went home that evening. Her mother responded that she would have accepted the invitation. This must have been in 1960 when Ted was divorced from his first wife and before he was serious with Lee, his second wife.

Neil Rosenthal was a young man living in the rural area of Highland Road where Ted lived. He would "Thumb a Ride" while walking on Highland Rd toward town. Ted picked him up many times in his Cadilac convertible and would ask him many questions about his activities, never about baseball. "He was just a nice guy giving me a ride."

Rhonda Goodwin, whom I met at COA, has a son, Joel (age 50+), who was an overnight Camper at age 8 in 1979. It cost $150 for one week - he stayed for 2 weeks. It cost too much to continue to send him overnight, but they did send him there daily for a couple of years after that. Cost? Rhonda's father disliked Ted because he was a "Draft Dodger" and away when his daughter Bobby-Jo was born. He evidently believed what the Boston Press were printing, which upset him so much. I corrected these incorrect thoughts and told her that Ted swore a lot. She said her father would have liked Ted for that because he was also profane.

Darryl J Bernier is a lifetime resident of Lakeville and a Member of the Park Commission after the town purchased the Camp property in 1986. He had meetings and is still in contact with Albert Cassidy Jr. in that capacity. He told me he was a Day Camper for 3 years for a week or two each year in the 1970s and 1980s. He attended at no charge because he was one of a few local boys who worked for free doing maintenance at the Park during the summer Camp season. Ted stayed in Alberts's house at the entrance to the Camp when he visited in the 1970s. When the Boy Scouts owned the property, Les Warburton used to vacation on the shore of Loon Pond with his family. There were three cottages opposite the dining hall when the Boy Scouts were active and another behind the Office, now used to store horseshoes. Three more cabins were added for dormitories of Campers when the Ted Williams Camp was established.

Ted Williams and his partners decided to end the Camp and sell the property in 1986 for $1.5M. A local entrepreneur had made an offer, which resulted in the town contracting for a formal professional appraisal. The town later took ownership by "eminent domain", paying the partners $2.6M for the property ($650K for each partner). The town Board of Selectmen sent Ted a letter on March 21, 1989, stating their intent to "keep the area as a recreational facility for youth and adults and would like to maintain his name on what had become generally known as the Ted

Williams Baseball Camp". He answered in his own handwriting on the return letter, "Permission Granted," with the understanding that he would be protected with a $1M insurance policy against his liability. A copy of the letter was posted in the Camp office today.

Alan Silliker attended the 2024 Ted Williams Alumni and Friends Jimmy Fund Reunion on July 13, 2024, at the Loon Lodge on the Ted Williams Camp property. He was a "Yellow Shirt" Jr Counselor in 1967 (See Photo) and a "White Shirt" Senior Counselor in 1968. The Camp had an infirmary with nursing at the Camp. His father was the Camp Doctor who visited active Camp sessions in the 1960s. He treated some Campers at his home close by. Bob Murray, an EMT, was head of the Infirmary and lived in a dormitory on-site during the active season.

The Camp offered (3) sessions in the 1970s - Two (4) weeks and One (3) weeks each for a total of (11)weeks. Al Cassidy, the Camp Executive Director, was seen frequently and demanded the high standards set originally by Ted. Alan sketched for me the arrangement of buildings scattered about in the Camp. He added that Ted, now single, rented a small house in the Cedardale Rd area of Long Pond in the summer of 1966. He and another Counselor later moved some of Ted's personal belongings to the house he purchased in 1967 on Marion Rd in Middleboro. There were boxes and trunks that were put in a locked bedroom on the second floor. They stayed there when Ted rented the house to Dennis and Joyce Gillette in 1969, and he left for Washington, D.C. Alan has a house on Pond Lane in the Cedardale area today. You drive by the small house Ted rented on Cedardale St before turning onto Pond Lane.

Viola Fairweather, whom I met at the COA, moved to Lakeville in 1996 and taught school for 26 years in Middleboro. At the age of 16, when living in Somerville, MA, she attended a 1956 New Year's Eve party at the home of friends of her parents living at Lucille Place, a very short dead-end street in Newton Highlands, MA. There were 30 friends and neighbours at home next to where Ted lived with friends. She was "In Awe!" when she danced with Ted Williams.

Hugh Rogers, owner of Capt. Bub's Marine on County Rd in Lakeville removed Bernie Cassidy's house, which used to run through his marina and is now used for boat storage, from the corner of Cassidy Lane. By coincidence, he formally owned Meehan Flower Shop (previously named Creeden's Flower Shop) on Center St in Middleboro. In the 1970s, when visiting his Boys Camp, Ted Williams often ordered flowers by phone to be sent to people all across the country." He was one of my best customers," although he never met Ted. He paid by credit card.

Roger Pinard, the current owner of J&J Seafood restaurant on County Rd., bought from Albert H. Cassidy the "Lakeview Drive-In" restaurant and renamed it in 1976. I made copies of 2 newspaper articles Roger gave me when I stopped to tell him of my effort to write this book. "Lakeview Drive-In offers Seafood Delights" and "Dining Out on the South Shore". He had never met Ted but was happy to say that he had been told that "Ted sat right over there many times" while pointing to a given table. Two ladies were having their meal while I was there. One spoke up to give me her story.

Nancy Lucas told me she was one of the "Cute Car-Hops" I had heard about. The above "regular people" and others were happy to provide me with stories which weaved the fabric of Ted's "Overlooked Legacy" created while living in Lakeville for 10 weeks every year from 1961 through 1968.

The Legacy continued after he left Lakeville to manage the Washington Senators Major Lague baseball team. He frequently visited Lakeville to assist his partners in supervising operations and adhering to the principles of discipline and character building until the Camp closed in 1986. He also ensured it was a "Fun" experience.

THE OVERLOOKED LEGACY OF TED WILLIAMS
continues July 13, 2024
"Ted Williams Camp Alumni & Friends -- Jimmy Fund Benifit"

Assembled at Loon Pond Lodge at the Ted Williams Camp, Lakeville, MA, with 22 Alumnai and 30 Friends enjoying a reunion with stories, silent auction games, door prizes and a buffet luncheon.

Pictured are the 22 Boys Baseball Camp and Girls Camp alumnai comimg from as far away as Colorado and New Hampshire, wearing the memento red cap.
Center front is the 2008 Alumnai originator and leader of this years semi-annual event, Joe LoRusso, with two girls representing the Girls Camp and the Office alumnai at his side.
This Jimmy Fundraiser is one of 4 events conducted in the area this year, raising over $10,000 including donations for the Dana Faber-Cancer Institute.

(8) Yellow Shirts (9) White Shirts	TOP ROW - Bob Heimswitz - Bill Timlin - Tim Adams - Pete Huey - Frank Boulton - Paul Cochrane John Thompson - Larry Ewing - Larry Diaz - Art Gillespie - Don Lowrey - Eddie Waitken Tom Padgen - Stan Thomas - Billy Parrat - Bob Murray Sr. - Joe Mach
(7) White Shirts	MIDDLE ROW - (White Shirts) Marty Esthner - Al Palmeiri - Roy Engle - Ted Williams (Black Shirt) Joe Comacho - John Motha - Bob Murray Jr. - Don Lambright
(10) Yellow Shirts	FRONT ROW - Cecil Kingsley - Alan Silliken - Don McMillan - Mark Davison - Mike Lynn - Bob Casey Stu Meadows - Chuck Sousa - Neil Olson - Skip Winters

TED WILLIAMS BOYS BASEBALL CAMP

LAKEVILLE, MA 1975

One of 10 teams in travel uniforms "Red Shirts" Joe Lorusso - Seated Front Row - 3rd from Right

TED WILLIAMS BOYS BASEBALL CAMP

LAKEVILLE, MA 1980's

6 Senior Counselors "White Shirts"

7 Junior Counselors "Yellow Shirts"

Joe LoRusso - Kneeling Front Row - 2nd from Left

Ted Williams Camp alumni carry on late slugger's legacy

2024

By Anna Milton | reporter@nemasketweek.com

LAKEVILLE — The rain wasn't going to get in the way of Paul Vieira's first visit back to the Ted Williams campground in 40 years.

Vieira, who lives in Colorado Springs, came back for an alumni reunion at Ted Williams Camp in Lakeville on Saturday, July 13.

Ted Williams Camp was a baseball camp co-founded by the Baseball Hall of Famer that operated from 1958 to 1986.

"I'm going to walk around, as soon as the rain stops, to see if I recognize things that I haven't seen in so many years," said Vieira. Vieira was a camper from 1975 to 1978.

The purpose of Saturday's event was two-fold, to serve as an alumni reunion as well as a fundraiser for the Jimmy Fund, which raises money for the Dana-Farber Cancer Institute. The Jimmy Fund was a charity near and dear to the baseball legend's heart.

Ted Williams Camp alumni get together for a reunion every two years, said Tina Murphy, who worked in the camp's office from 1980 to -1985.

This year, returning alumni received something special: a Ted Williams Camp hat.

The camp was a breeding ground for baseball skills and lifelong friendships, which was clear in the strong handshakes, smiles and exchanges as alumni reminisced about shared experiences as campers, coaches and staff members of the institution.

Some, like Vieira and David Boyle, journeyed several hours to come to the event. Boyle, who was a camper from 1965 to 1967, came down from Franconia, New Hampshire with his son and two grandchildren.

This was his first reunion. "Just to be back in the area, get the hat, bring the grandkids," was "great" he said.

The trip down memory lane led him to recall the unfortunate fate of the two baseballs he got Ted Williams to autograph, something that took him two years to work up the courage to ask for.

He would later find his brother had put them to good use out in the field without asking permission, he said.

July 13, 2024

About 50 people attended Saturday's event, said Joe LoRusso, who founded the alumni group in 2008 and spearheads fundraising efforts for the Jimmy Fund.

Through admission fees, a silent auction and donations, the alumni group hopes to present a check of over $10,000 to the Jimmy Fund next month, said LoRusso.

The reunion gave Paul Vieira an opportunity to reminisce about when he got the chance to meet Ted Williams himself.

"I think that was probably the memory that I remember the best. Seeing Ted out there telling you: 'you need to level out that bat a little bit', or something like that, that was cool," he said.

Baseball coach Earl Mathewson said interactions with Ted Williams are also precious memories for him. Mathewson served as Director of Baseball Operations at the camp for the last five years the camp was open, from 1980-1985.

Mathewson said those one-on-one meetings where Williams gave him coaching tips stuck with him.

"Ted Williams was my Aristotle in baseball," he said. "There was nobody better."

Saturday's reunion was the fourth fundraiser this year put on by the Ted Williams Camp alumni, and the group has already raised $9,000 for the Jimmy Fund, according to LoRusso.

LoRusso said he feels Ted Williams would approve of how the group is continuing his legacy of supporting the Jimmy Fund.

"I bet he'd look down at us and say: 'I'm proud of you people and what you're doing,'" he said.

Former campers Dave Boyle, left, and Paul Vieira. Photos by Anna Milton

Earl Mathewson holds up his bio from when he served as head coach at the camp as well as photos of him with Ted Williams.

Joe LoRusso, left, and Steve Ferroli. Ferroli has run the Ted Williams/ Steve Ferroli baseball program for over 40 years.

View more photos online at nemasketweektoday.com

Ted Williams and a young patient

"During his lifetime, Ted was uncomfortable when praised for all he did for the Jimmy Fund," says Edward J. Benz Jr., MD, President Emeritus. "But, let me say now that his commitment to the Jimmy Fund and to the children facing cancer should go in the record books as among the most any professional athlete has done to advance a cause."

"Ted signed on for life to the Jimmy Fund, helping make it the best-loved charity in New England," adds Mike Andrews, former Boston Red Sox second baseman and chairman of the Jimmy Fund. "Ted's name is synonymous with our battle against cancer."

THE OVERLOOKED LEGACY CONTINUES

Joel Slutsky was a three week camper at the end of July in both years 1972 and 1973. He received scholarships of $75 and $50 these years toward a college education in his future. The Cover letters congratulating him were signed by The Lakeville Baseball Camp Inc. , Bernard J. Cassidy, Trustee and Director of the Camp. The context of the award was sent in another letter:

"To the Parents, Friends, Campers, Staff, and Business Associates who have so generously donated to our NINTH ANNUAL SCHOLARSHIP DRIVE, THANK YOU sincerely for your help and support. To the Trustees of the Foundation, Mr. Wallace Wilkie and Mr. Ellis Phillips our heartfelt appreciation for devoting their time and effort in the difficult task of selecting the boys to be awarded these scholarships.

It is our hope that in some small way these awards will stimulate the boys to prepare themselves for a higher education. Although some boys do not need the financial help, it is possible that an award might provide them with an incentive to do better academically. The winners are selected on the basis of Conduct, Leadership, Attitude, & Sportsmanship, not only on the diamonds but in all around camp activities."

LAKEVILLE BASEBALL CAMP, INC.
Lakeville, Mass. 02346

TEL. 617 - 947-0726

August 10, 1973

Joel Slutsky
868 Hereford Way
Schenectady, N. Y. 12309

Dear Joel:

CONGRATULATIONS! You have been chosen to receive one of the Ted Williams Camp College Scholarship awards in the amount of $50.00.

During your stay at camp your coaches, counselors, and the administration wrote a number of evaluations on you and on all other campers. On the basis of these evaluations, a non-partisan Board of Directors voted the scholarship awards.

The money will be held in escrow in the United National Bank of Taunton. As per ouf Indenture of Trust you qualify to receive this money when we are notified that you are enrolled "in any college, university, or other institution of higher learning of your choice in the United States or elsewhere, including professional schools."

Through the awarding of this scholarship, we hope to encourage you to pursue the perfection of your mind as you have sought to gain the perfection of your athletic ability.

Congratulations again, and best of luck to you in the school year ahead.

Sincerely,

Bernard J. Cassidy

Wallace Wilkie, Chairman
Ellis Philips, Trustee
Bernard J. Cassidy, Trustee

DIRECTORS: Ted Williams Albert Cassidy Bernard Cassidy Lester Warburton

Joel Slutsky provided the color photo of Ted Williams in front of more than 45 young campers, counselors and coaches seated on the grass playing field. Ted is listening to a brave boy expressing his thoughts on the subject of Baseball Basics - probably hitting strategy ?

Ted, listening intently while leaning on his bat, is providing a learning experience which every camper remembers and took home as a meaningful time at camp.

Joel was one of many campers who received college scholarships because of his positive participation at the Lakeville Baseball Camp.

Awards were made to campers who played well at one of the 9 positions at each of the 4 diamonds and to a "Utility" position (Umpire?)

Awards were also made to campers for - Most Hustle, Most Improved, Best Base Runner, Most Coachable, Best All Around, and Most Valuable Player.

"Scholarships were made on the basis of CONDUCT, LEADERSHIP ATTITUDE and SPORTSMANSHIP not only on the baseball diamond but in all around camp activities." Some were recognized as "Hall of Famers".

The "Overlooked Legacy of Ted Williams" is encapsulated in the above.

The devoted hard work, loyality and integrity of Teds partners, Albert H. Cassidy, Bernard J. Cassidy and Lester Warburton and their wives, year round for 30 years is also a Legacy that should not be Overlooked
It was done with a "Handshake" in 1957 and ended in 1986.

CHAPTER 15

TED LEAVES LAKEVILLE 1969 - 1986

The decision was made. A very emotional one! Ted left Lakeville and his Boys Baseball Camp in January 1969 with his third wife Deloris and their baby son John Henry.

On Feb 1, 1969, Ted assumed a new career as manager of the Washington Senators, a struggling major league baseball team. He was also leaving a recently purchased home in Middleboro, MA, renting it to Dennis and Joyce Gillette with the thought that he might return. He had no managerial experience with a major league team. It was a high-risk opportunity with significant financial benefits and a chance to create an organization that fit his style and with open-ended authority to build a team. The position was given by the new owner, Bob Short, anxious to have the legendary Ted Williams as its leader.

The operating management of the Boys' Baseball Camp was in good hands. The three partners, Albert, Bernie, and Lester, had the process under control. They expanded the summer sessions to 11 weeks, thus maximising the income. They continued to improve the facilities and create new experiences for the Campers. They made it a disciplined yet fun experience for as many as 150 Campers each year.

On January 22, 1970, the Middleboro Gazette printed the following news article. "Request by Albert Cassidy for a land and gravel permit was withdrawn by him at a hearing before Lakeville selectmen after 27 area residents registered opposition." After the hearing, Albert said their intention was to "Improve the Camp property - We had no idea how the folks in our neighbourhood felt about the hill". The selectmen thanked Albert with the statement" -"Again, we are shown the Cassidys are civic-minded."

Beginning in 1958, the TED WILLIAMS CAMP management sent a "Personal Report Card" to each Camper at the end of the season under the direction of Albert H. Cassidy, the Executive Director. The tradition of reporting a Camper's Progress continued until 1986, when the Camp ended. A cover letter written in the 1970s by the then Executive Director, Bernard J. Cassidy, clearly states that the mission of providing a meaningful experience never changed.

The Red Sox maintained their Spring Training site continuously from 1968 to 1992 for 24 years in Winter Haven, Florida. This is where Albert H. Cassidy moved with his family in 1970. Ted and the Cassidy family often visited the Spring Training.

On one occasion during 1973 Spring Training, he chastised a new Red Sox player, Dwight Evans. Dwight recounts, "A horrible first meeting with Ted when I was a twenty-year-old. He used adjectives I had never heard of before - actually inventing new swear words. The ballpark was quiet except for the sound of Ted's booming voice, which really gave it to me. It was my worst nightmare... I didn't talk to Ted for four years after that." Dwight Evans went on to have a very successful career with the Red Sox and was honoured in Ted's Museum and Hitters Hall of Fame" in Citrus Hills, Florida. He recently published a book "Dewey - Behind the Gold Glove, and went on to explain, "I came around to thinking Ted was a neat guy".

Ref: Dan Shaughnessy Boston Globe August 25, 2024 Sports Section C.

"Catching up with great Yastrzemski at 85."

Ted coached Yaz by phone in 1961 while in his office at the Ted Williams Boys Baseball Camp in Lakeville. Ted was active with Red Sox sports while developing his "Overlooked Legacy" in Lakeville.

Ted would return every summer from 1969 - 1986 for a couple of weeks to oversee the Boys Baseball Camp operation, making himself known and promoting his hitting philosophy. Those campers lucky enough to see and listen to Ted always remembered the occasion, as well as his riding around in a golf cart, which had replaced his bicycle.

Ted would stay with Bernie Cassidy and his family in the house at the camp's entrance with his son John Henry, a teenager who would participate as a Camper during these visits.

The house he purchased in 1967 in Middleboro was rented to Dennis and Joyce Gillette in early 1969 when he moved to Washington, D.C., to manage the Washington Senators baseball team. He sold it to them in September 1975. He lived there with his wife Deloris in 1968. Their son John Henry was born in Vermont in 1968 and lived with them there for a few months.

When Ted left, his personal effects, memorabilia, and souvenirs were moved into a locked second-floor bedroom. He never returned to recover them. The local Real Estate salesman had the keys to the locked room and opened it after the property was sold to the Dennises in 1975.

The salesman had Ted's personal items removed and stored at an unknown location in Lakeville (probably on the Camp site?), until 1986, when the town of Lakeville purchased the Camp.

In 1994, the "Ted Williams Museum and Hitters Hall of Fame" was opened in Citrus Hills, Florida. They requested Lakeville to provide items for the museum if possible. Lakeville town officials sent a lot of items to them. At this time, Lakeville also offered boxes of items to residents. Peter Chiuppi of Lakeville obtained one box containing the Red Junior Campers T-shirt and copies of the Baseball Basics brochure, as well as a handout to every Camper when they arrived at Camp. They are pictured at the end of Chapter 10.

The Florida Museum closed in 2007, and many items were moved to the Tampa Bay Rays Tropicana Field in St. Petersburg, Florida, where a museum of baseball memorabilia is on display today. Some baseball items, as well as his fishing and Marine Pilots items, got lost in the move.

One of the new Campers, Joe LoRusso, an 11-year-old in 1975, was sent to the Ted Williams Baseball Camp by his parents because the YMCA camp he attended in New Hampshire closed. His father worked at the Sears Roebuck Corporate office, down the street from Fenway Park in Boston, where he would see Ted Williams walk through the door when he was their sports advisor. Joe's father read in a Boston newspaper that Ted ran a baseball camp in Lakeville, MA. Thus, he found a new home for his son, a sports enthusiast.

Joe remembers having a bad day at bat when a voice from behind the home plate screen told him, "Hey, Kid, keep your eye on the ball". It was one of those infrequent days that Ted would now visit the Camp yet interject himself with a boy who needed encouragement. Joe was in awe that it was Ted Williams speaking directly to him. Ted later took him aside and gave him a personal lesson on hitting. Joe loved his Camp experience and often returned until he was injured during a game by an errant pitch, shattering his left elbow.

In the 1980's he became a "Yellow Shirt" Jr. Counselor passing on Ted's philosophy on hitting.

(See 1975 photo of Camper Joe in a "Red Shirt" sitting in the front row, 3rd in from the right end and later, a 1980 photo of Joe as a Jr. Counselor kneeling 2nd from left end in the front row, dressed as a Junior Counselor in a "Yellow Shirt."

OTHER ALUMNI REPORTED THEIR PERSONAL EXPERIENCES;

Mitchell Grespico: "I went in 1977. I was a good hitter and became a great hitter. It was a great experience for me."

Jeff Connell: "I went in the summer of 1970. Great memories. Coach Ken Nosek and dorm. Counsellor "Yellow Shirt" Steve Slocum. Two ball games a day. Lots of salt tablets, the lake, batting cages, a giant picture of Ted hitting, hanging in the dining hall, the canteen after supper, reveille and taps, trips to Lincoln Park and Fenway. Ted, as manager of the Senators, waving to us in the grandstand above the visitor's dugout and the long canvas TWC sign."

Bob Kirkendale to Jeff Connell: "You didn't mention Tetherball, and I missed the bus returning to camp."

Geoffrey S. Mendall: I ran the waterfront in '68 & '69.

Frank Ward: "I attended TWC from 1959 to 1963 and remember it fondly. I pitched for the 1959 undefeated LL team in a charity game at Kelly Field in Hyde Park, MA. The following seasons I moved up to the big diamond and played in the New Bedford Twilight League game."

Bob Kirkendale: " I went to Ted Williams Camp from 1969 - 1972. I pitched every year. Jeff Vunkle won the award for best pitcher in his league. I then decided to win the award. The next year, I struck out 21 batters in one game and won that award."

Hank Seaman: Writer for the Standard-Times of New Bedford - July 6, 2003

"It doesn't seem possible a year has gone by since the death of Ted Williams. But, then, I can hardly believe it's been 40 summers since I counselled at this Lakeville baseball camp. Those two years at Ted Williams Camp -- 1962-63 -- were, without a doubt, the two most glorious summers a baseball-besotted teen could have wished for. I couldn't resist riding out to Lakeville this past week to see the old campgrounds.

The town has taken over the camp for various recreational activities, so while it has indisputably changed, it is still recognisably the camp of my memories. There was the same short ride from the Lakeville Town Hall to the camp's tree-lined entrance on Precinct St. Pangs hit me hard when I saw the unmistakable yet somewhat changed former mess hall.

I clearly picture Les Warburton and his brothers-in-law Al and Bernie Cassidy—the camp's owners in partnership with Ted—conferring at a mess table with top assistants Al Palmieri, Joe Camacho, and John Motha.

A better group of mentors than you'd ever meet, each treating campers and counsellors alike with fairness and respect. Heading right at what used to be the camp's office, I was saddened to see the "Snack Shack" gone, and beyond that, the area that used to house batting cages is now bare ground. Heading down the road, it didn't take long to realise a series of horseshoe pits had replaced the dorm cabins. An immediate picture of long-ago evenings when groups of us would play the then-new game of Wiffleball on this very spot. Further down on what used to be the road to the original dorm cabins is now a fenced-off skateboard park opposite a work shed. And a basketball court. Across the way are soccer pitches, not to mention what looks like volleyball sand pits. in different capacities -- and they could fill volumes. Ted, larger than life, pedalled his bike for the entire length and breadth of camp. In a Jimmy Fund contest, Ted is hitting a "Blooper Ball" out of sight. Ted and fellow Hall of Famer Hank Greenberg compare notes in the batting cage.

But, most of all, I have memories of Ted Williams taking a liking to an impressionable, tongue-tied teen and teaching him a thing or two about life -- lessons still with that no-longer-young boy all these decades later."

And better yet, I have recollections of Ted Williams on each field -- Albert H. Cassidy left Lakeville with his family in 1970 to settle in Winter Haven, Florida, leaving the management of the Camp to Bernie and Lester. Albert was ill. Ted brought him to Boston to see his doctor, who tested Albert, and he was advised to move south to a climate that would help him recover. The Camp continued the Legacy of Ted from 1969 until its closing in 1986, even though Ted and his original partner, Albert, were no longer living in Lakeville.

One last memory of an alumni sums up the Camp experiences of the more than 10,000 young men who attended the Ted Williams Boys Baseball Camp for the 28 years of its existance. And the 1000 young women who attended the Girls Day Camp during the same period.

Joe Moran: "I was in the very last week of the Camp in 1986 and had a fantastic time. I learned so much in that one week that it helped me play in high school and eventually in college. I wish I had gone to the camp earlier."

THE LEGACY CONTINUES!

PHOTO TOUR OF EXISTING LAKEVILLE TED WILLIAMS CAMP

LEFT: Original Dining Hall
RIGHT: Original Office
MIDDLE: Original Flag Pole
REAR: Woods and Loon Pond

Little League Ball Field
Background:
Dining Hall & Office
Home Plate:
2 LL Baseball Bats
& Blooper Ball

ORIGINAL
Concession Stand
Located Between
4 Ball Fields

PHOTO TOUR OF EXISTING LAKEVILLE TED WILLIAMS CAMP

One of 5
Ball Fields
each
with
2 Dug-Outs

Looking into
Little League
Dug-Out
with
Bat & Blooper Ball

Looking out
from
Little League
Dug-Out
with
2 Bats & Blooper Ball

PHOTO TOUR OF EXISTING LAKEVILLE TED WILLIAMS CAMP

INFORMATION BULLETIN BOARD AND SITE MAP OF BALL FIELDS IN BACKGROUND

"LOON POND LODGE" WAS ORIGINALLY THE BOY SCOUT AND THEN THE BOYS BASEBALL DINING HALL

PRECINCT ST ENTRANCE TO TED WILLIAMS CAMP

A HOUSE WAS MOVED TO THE SITE- LIVED IN BY PARTNER ALBERT H. CASSIDY AND FAMILY - LATER DESTROYED

PHOTO TOUR OF EXISTING LAKEVILLE TED WILLIAMS CAMP

Original: Batting Practice Enclosures with old netting
Original: 2 Practice Pitching Mounds with Home Plates

One of 4: Major League Ball Fields with Limited Bench Seating
Behind Fencing along 1st & 3rd Base Lines
and Tall Netting behind Home Plate

CHAPTER 16

END CAMP - LEGACY CONTINUES

"In 1991, on the fiftieth anniversary of his .406 year, Harvard University wanted to give him an Honorary Degree, but he turned it down, feeling that he would have been out of place among the intelligence in Harvard Yard."

TED'S INTEGRITY LINGERS

Joe Lorusso, an early Camper and later Staff Counselor, recognized that it would be good to welcome Campers back for a reunion experience. In 2008, he organized the first "Alumni and Friends" event. It was an all-day affair with many activities: a silent auction of related items and local services, games, a buffet luncheon, and the appearance of a retired Red Sox player.

100 "Boys," now adult men who were Campers in the 1950s, '60s, '70s, and '80s, came from around the country to attend. He also took the opportunity to continue Ted's support of the Jimmy Fund, offering the proceeds of the event and other donations to the Jimmy Fund, Dana Faber Cancer Hospital.

Joe continued to organise the event every other year until the 2019 COVID-19 epidemic prevented holding such an event. He revitalized the event on July 13, 2024, which attracted 30 plus alumni plus 20 friends with a smaller, shorter yet duplicate event at the same Loon Pond Lodge on the existing Ted Williams Camp property. The number of alumni is getting smaller as the years go by, but the enthusiasm continues.

Another friend and dedicated attendee was Joanne Warburton Mecke, the daughter of one of the original partners, Lester Warburton. She still lives in a nearby town. She was active as a young girl, working with her parents, uncles, and aunts in operating the Camp from the beginning. She was even able to take advantage of the Girl's Day Camp activities when she was in her teens.

Selected commentary by staff writer John Tessier for the New Bedford Standard-Times - South Coast Today article of August 14, 2008, adds to the "Overlooked Legacy of Ted Williams." He wrote:

"In 1958, Ted Williams Camp was opened to campers ages 7-17 for two —to three-week overnight sessions. Campers played baseball games and received instruction all day. Ted gave them advice on their swing.

Joe LoRusso, who spent 11 years at the Ted Williams Camp as both a camper and a member of the coaching staff, decided to celebrate those memories by throwing a reunion celebration last Sunday.

Ted Williams was requested in the following 1989 letter by the Town of Lakeville for their permission to use his name in the future for the property. He agrees!

OFFICE OF SELECTMEN

Town of Lakeville
346 Bedford Street
Lakeville, Mass. 02347
March 21, 1989

If T. W's name is used the town will need to notify our ins. company to list him as a co-insured on our liability pol. for at least one million dollars.
BJP 4/24/89

Mr. Ted Williams
Courtesy of Lester J. Warburton
2013-24 San Marcos Drive, S.E.
Winter Haven, FL 33880

Dear Mr. Williams:

As you may be aware, the Town of Lakeville is now the owner of the former Ted Williams Baseball Camp property. The transfer of ownership was arranged by a friendly eminent domain taking after being overwhelmingly approved by voters at a town meeting in 1986.

It is the intention of the Board of Selectmen to keep the area as a recreational facility for youth as well as adults. The baseball fields have been re-done and are ready for use this year; there is a jogging trail planned; also a picnic area and the possibility of a fishing pier at pondside.

Up to a short time ago we had not given serious thought to a name for the facility because it was always referred to by everyone as the Ted Williams Baseball Camp. Now, however, we feel it is time to select a name and would like to know if you would allow us the honor to call it the Ted Williams Recreational Facility in the Town of Lakeville. We feel that name would be most appropriate and hope for your response in the affirmative.

Your kind consideration of our request will be appreciated, and if you choose to grant it will you please acknowledge permission below.

Permission granted with the understanding that I will be co-insured on a liability policy with limits no less than $1,000,000.00. Name automatically withdrawn if not insured. T.S.W.

Permission granted March 31, 1989

Ted Williams

Very truly yours,
Lakeville Board of Selectmen

By *Richard A. Fickert*
Richard A. Fickert

George F. Rose
George F. Rose

F. James Healey
F. James Healey

RAF:BJP

THIS STORY NEEDED TO BE TOLD

THE END

The "Ted Williams Camp" continues to be a town-owned public facility in Lakeville, MA.

The coaches got up, 6-10 of them, and told stories. Pat Dunn, another camper and coach in attendance, travelled 1800 miles from Sarasota, Florida. He spoke glowingly about his time there.

- "These were the best years of our lives" --- Mr. Dunn said he learned a lot during his tenure at the camp --- "I learned a lot more than just how to play baseball here; I learned life lessons." He went on to explain how the leadership skills and life lessons he picked up at the Ted Williams Camp transferred over into his professional life.

Steve Ferrolli, whose time at the Ted Williams Camp left a lasting impression, is now an instructor in the Ted Williams League in Hanson, MA, left with a memory few baseball fans can top. --- Steve actually got to debate Ted's theory of hitting with the legend, with the two discussing angles of pitching using sticks and strings to illustrate their points. They stayed in touch over the years. --- "Ted actually flew me to his house in Florida. He sat me down at his kitchen table and said -- "Do you know who teaches my theories on hitting better than anyone ?" I said -- "no" --- He said -- "You do" "--- and you are going to carry on my legacy."

"The Ted Williams League uses the theory of one of the best hitters in baseball history to teach hitting. The League (Camp) is for people from ages 5-50 and is about to go into national duplication." (It is an active day camp today in Hanson. Steve attended the July 13, 2024, Alumna Ted Williams and Friends Jimmy Fund party in Lakeville.)

"The memories and lessons taught at the Camp live on in the Ted Williams League as well as in the lives of those who were fortunate enough to spend a few weeks in the summer playing America's favourite pastime with a Boston legend."

Hopefully, Joe can keep up the good work with another Jimmy Fund event two years from now.

EPILOGUE

Ted gave to himself, achieving his lifetime goal of being "The Greatest Hitter Who Ever Lived." He gave to his country in peace and in war when called upon. He did his best in everything he attempted, including his love for his wives and children. His DNA, however, prevented him from ever settling down in what would be considered a normal life to most people. He lived out of a suitcase most of his life, traveling with a professional baseball team for six months for 13 years while renting space in a hotel or living in basic military quarters for six years.

According to his third wife, Delores, he considered three locations where he owned property to be his home, all simultaneously: In the winter, the Keys in Florida. The Miramichi River in New Brunswick, Canada, in the spring and fall. It was in Lakeville, MA, for 10 weeks every summer for 8 years and for a total of 29 years that he gave of himself for the betterment of young boys and girls. They became better people because of the positive, disciplined lives they shared with others from all over the world. Three local regular families, all related, became equal partners with a handshake from Ted in the creation and operation of a Boys Baseball Camp.

Albert H. Cassidy and his wife Kathleen, Bernard and his wife Theresa (Terry) and Lester Warburton and his wife Ethel Mae (Cassidy), and their children all participated in the operation of The Ted Williams Boys Baseball Camp. Ted set the standard and funded it until it became self-sufficient. The partners benefited because they demanded of themselves loyal leadership with integrity throughout the life of the Camp.

Lester J. Warburton and his wife Ethel Cassidy Warburton are buried in the Samson Cemetery on Bedford St. Lester was a US Navy Submarine EM2 Sailor during WWII. The crew of the USS Sailfish were awarded a Presidential Citation for their success patrolling in the Pacific Ocean.

The cemetery property was part of the total property sold to the Ted Williams Baseball Camp before it was donated to a private group in 1944 by the Boston Council of Boy Scouts. Thus the Warburtons continue to be part of the Camp after working tirelessly for 30 years (1957-1986) as partners in the ownership and management of the Ted Williams Camp.

The devoted hard work, loyalty and integrity of Ted's partners Albert H. Cassidy, Bernard J. Cassidy and Lester J. Warburton and their wives for 30 years is also a legacy that should not be overlooked. It was done with a handshake in 1957 and ended with the sale of the property to the Town of Lakeville in 1986.

A recent phone call from Albert B. Cassidy, the son of Albert H.Cassidy the originator of the Boys Camp, said, "They owe their success in developing a major real estate business in Winter Haven, FL to their experience living and working in Lakeville, MA. and working with Ted Williams. They all worked as a team in a happy and positive atmosphere. Never an argument."

They had FUN!

Ted asked Albert B. Cassidy to be the executor of his estate when he died. Albert accepted the request. He was born in 1957 when the Boy Scouts purchased the Camp property. He was a Camper until age 13, when his father moved the family to Florida in 1970 at the suggestion of his (and Ted's) doctor for health reasons. Thus, Albert experienced many of the relationships Ted had with his family and the many ball players who were Ted's friends.

The Ted Williams Boys Baseball Camp also carried on his long-time active support of the Jimmy Fund. It continues to this day in Lakeville, MA.

THE LEGACY THAT SHOULD NOT BE "OVERLOOKED"

TED WILLIAMS BOOK AUTHORIZATIONS

I wish to thank the following people who gave me their stories and encouraged me to write the story of the "Overlooked Legacy of Ted Williams". They all seemed to be happy to find an outlet of their memories to be documented. It has been a fulfilling experience.

1 ROAN BARBER
2 MARY STANDISH
3 WILFORD COREY
4. DIANE TISDALE
5 MARGRET (PEG) GROSS (GILBERT)
6 JANET MURPHY
7 FRED CORREIA
8 JOYCE GILLETTE
9 PETER CHIUPPI
10 BRUCE BAPTISTE
11 LEO ROUSSEAU
12 NANCY A JOHNSON LAFAVE
13 ANNE HIGGINS
14 RHONDA GOODWIN
15 NEIL ROSENTHAL
16 DARRYL J BERNIER
17 BILL MARKSON
18 FRADA MARVEL
19 VIOLA FAIRWEATHER
20 LESTER GARNIER
21 MARILYN J. DORSEY
22 HUGH J. ROGERS
23 PAUL A. GUSTAFSON
24 JOSEPH LORUSSO
25 ROBERT DENISE
26 JOANNE WARBURTON MECKE
27 CLAIRE & PAUL DUMAS
28 DOUGLAS BERRY
29 JEFFREY CONNELL
30 FRANK WARD
31 ALAN SILLIKER
32 GLEN J PINA
33 FRED BROWN
34 RACHEL COLLINS

A SPECIAL THANK YOU

LIBBY FOX, the Reference and Adult Services Librarian of the City of Middleboro Public Library provided me with the much-valued retrieval of articles from the Middleboro Gazette newspaper printed during the period that the Ted Williams Boys Baseball Camp existed. These articles were filmed and placed in the library's computer-based system. She located and printed them for me.

This book would not have been possible without her able and dedicated service.

Thank you, Libby and the Middleboro Library.

This is to thank the many people who provided enthusiastic support by telling of their experiences and providing documentation defining the "Overlooked Legacy of Ted Williams". Thirty-four signed an Authorization form, and many more people came forward wishing to contribute. Contacts were made frequently at chance meetings at various locations in the area and during the Friday morning coffee hour at the local Council on Aging facility on the Ted Williams Campgrounds. Other contacts were made during the Alumni and Friends reunion and Jimmy Fund Benefit at the Loon Pond Lodge, also located at the Ted Williams Camp, on July 13, 2024.

They all made this book possible.

REFERENCES

MG MIddleboro Gazette newspaper mm/dd/yy

R 1 THE KID Ben Bradlee 2013
Back Bay Books / Little, Brown and Company
Hachette Book Group
1290 Avenue of the Americas, New York, NY
10104 littlebrown.com

R2 WINGMEN Adam Lazarus 2023
Kensington Press Corp 119 West 40th St
NewcYork, NY 10018

R5 My Turn at Bat The Story of My Life 1969
by Ted Williams
As Told to John Underwood
SIMON AND SCHUSTER
ROCKEFELLER CENTER 630 FIFTH AVE
NEW YORK, NEW YORK 10020

R7 TED WILLIAMS LEIGH MONTVILLE 2004
FIRST ANCHOR BOOKS (BROADWAY BOOKS)
EDITION, 2005
division of Random House, Inc
New York, in 2004

R8 TED WILLIAMS Baseball Legends RICK WOLFF 1993
CHELSEA HOUSE PUBLISHERS
a division of Main Line Book Co
printed and bound in the United States of America

TED WILLIAMS LEGACY - TIME LINE

1918 - Ted born
1938 - Ted joins Red Sox - Sarasota to Minneapolis MN/Princeton Minor League
1939 - Ted met Doris Soule Princeton, MN - (1st wife)
- Ted played first year Red Sox Major League Fenway Park
1940 - Selective Service and Training Act created Sept 16
1941 - US enters WWII -US declares war/Japan Dec 8 - war/Germany & Italy Dec 11
1941 - Ted classified 1A Jan - late draft Number
1941 - Ted - Record - .406 Batting average end of season
1942 - Ted re-classified Draft Board to 3A in Feb
- Ted enlists in the US Navy in May - Pilot Training Program (Not Drafted)
1944 - Ted completes Training - Lt in US Marines - His choice
- Ted married Doris Soule - Pensacola, FL (dated for 5 years)
1946 - Ted released Marines active duty - reservist
- Ted Rejoins Red Sox - $40K/yr (4 years lost playing for Red Sox)
1948 - Ted becomes father to Barbra Joyce "Bobby-Jo" - Boston
- Boston Braves sponsor Jimmy Fund - Ted becomes active in support
1949 - Ted signs with Red Sox - $90K/yr
- Ted begins fishing Florida Keys
1950 - Ted fractures elbow - All-Star game-continues play-later operation-remove fragments
- Ted demonstrates fishing at Sportsman Show Boston Fall - 1 week $10K
- North invaded South Korea - the US sponsored a "Police Action" response
1952 - Ted recalled active duty - Marine Fighter Pilot
- Ted to South Korea - near-death crash-landing following hit over South Korea
- Ted becomes "Wingman" for John Glenn and a life-long friend
1953 - Ted discharged from active duty with awards - Police action in Korea ended in July
- Ted rejoins the Red Sox - again (2 years lost playing for Red Sox
- Assumes sponsor for Jimmy Fund for Red Sox - Braves leave Boston
1954 - Ted signs with Red Sox for $100K/yr
- Ted divorced Doris (married 10 years)
1957 - Ted appears yearly at Sports man Show Boston - Fly and Reel Casting - Fishing
- Ted accepts the invitation - goes to Miramachi River, New Brunswick, Canada- Fishing

- Ted meets Albert H. Cassidy in Fenway Park and accepts an invitation to Visit Lakeville

- Ted agrees to support the purchase of Scout Camp and the creation Boys Baseball Camp Meets with three partners - funds purchase - defines goals with a handshake.

Albert H. Cassidy - Executive Director Age 41

Bernard J Cassidy - Clerk - Age 39 Ted Age 39

Lester Warburton - (Brother-in-Law) - Age 38

(Ted retires from the Red Sox in 3 years - and leaves Camp management to partners)

- Albert B.Cassidy born to Albert H. and Ethel Cassidy

1958 - Ted becomes a member - of Miramichi River Anglers Asso - New Brunswick, Canada

- June 3 - Ted Williams Boys Baseball Camp - Open House - Lakeville, MA

- June 28 - Baseball Camp opening weekend - Ted presents both events

- TWC moves Garrish House from Loon Pond to Camp entrance on Precinct St.

1959 - Ted's neck in traction - Batting Avg drops to .254

- Ted requests salary drops from $125K to $90K

1960 - Teds last year as a player for the Red Sox

- Ted signs 5-year contract - Sears Roebuck – Mgr. Sports Advisory Group - $125K/Yr

- Ted dates Lee Howard of Chicago - Socialite

- Joanne Warburton, daughter of Lester and Ethel (Cassidy) - born

1961 - Ted built the new White Birch Lodge on Miramichi River

- Ted coaches Spring Training Red Sox - Arizona

- Ted attends first-year Boys Camp - Summer - full time

- Ted meets Lydia Rotch, owner of a large estate, Lakeville - Stonehouse & Guest- House.

- Albert H. Cassidy Mgr. Ops. Camp, Bernie/wife control $, Lester Mgr. Camp Maint.

- Ted marries Lee Howard /Fall - Honeymoon in Canada, Winter in Florida Keys - (dated for 2 years)

1962 - Ted & Lee live in Rotch Guest House on her Estate - Supervise Boys Camp

- Camp expanded to include girls "Hill Top Camp" - Stonehouse - Rotch Estate

- Carol Cassidy's daughter Albert H. attends Girls Hill Top Girls Camp - Stonehouse, Age 7

- John M. Cassidy b. 1936 - Bro of Albert H - lives on Precint St

1963 - Ted's daughter Bobby Jo visits Ted & Lee - and becomes a girl's "Day Camper"

1964 - January-Albert H. Cassidy purchases house/lot at Camp entrance moves in w/family

- Ted dedicates Lakeville Ball Field - Vaughn St - Plays Blooper Ball vs locals

1965 - Ted renews contract with Sears Roebuck for another 5 years - $125K/yr

1966 - Ted inducted into the Baseball Hall of Fame - interrupts summer supervision of Camp

- Ted divorced from Lee (Howard) - second wife (5 years married)
- Ted's daughter Bobby Jo - 18 - married and pregnant - had an abortion

1967 - Ted -"unmarried", purchases house Marion Rd, Sept 27, Middleboro (Plans to stay?)

- Ted moves personal belongings & memorabilia into a locked bedroom on 2nd floor

1968 - Deloris Wettach of VT – a girlfriend of Ted, became pregnant by Ted

- Ted marries Deloris May 7 (friends for 3 years)
- Son John Henry, born Aug 26
- Deloris helps decorate their house in Middleboro but delivers the baby in VT

1969 - Ted signs as Mgr. Washington Senators - Feb 29 Owner- Short heavily persuaded him with $1M plus benefits and control - Reluctant, then open - supported by Deloris. They move to Washington

- Ted's Sears Roebuck contract expires - In need of income.
- Lester & d. Joanne picked up Ted at Logan Airport from Washington Ted at their home for 1 week - County St

1970 - Ted rents Middleboro House (with contents) to Gillette

- Albert H. Cassidy moves to Winter Haven, FL with family/ Poor health - Doc recommend
- Bernie/Terry & Lester/Ethel ran Camp until it closed in 1986
- Ted visits Camp every summer for a week or two until it closed
- Camp now 11 weeks (was 8) signs up to 175 (est.?) Campers and is profitable.

1971 - Claudia b. Oct 8 - dau. of Ted and Delores in Washington

- Washinton Senators move to Texas as the Rangers

1972 - Ted resigns from Texas Rangers after 4 years of 5-year contract. Remains as an advisor.

1975 - Ted sells Middleboro house to Gillettes. Personal contents locked on the second floor were removed by the realtor and given to the town of Lakeville.

(Some mementoes were delivered in 1994 to the new Ted Williams Museum in Hernando, FL. Some were offered for free to any locals interested. Included were copies of the booklet Baseball Basics and a red Jr. Camper "T" shirt)

- Ted lived with his old friend Louise Kaufman from 1958 until she died in 1993 (18 years)

1975 - 1986 - Ted visits Lakeville every summer for a week or two to check up on the Camp. Lucky Campers remember his visits. Joe LoRusso included.

1982 & 1983 - Ted visited his son John Henry, a student at Eagle Brook Academy, a prep school, in Deerfield. MA. David Heritagem, Exec. Account Manager of PACIRA Biosciences, Inc. met Ted there a couple times.

- Ted brought John Henry to Lakeville during his summer visits. John would be a Camper when Ted visited. John went on to become a pro ball player.

1986 - Camp closes - sold for $2.6M Lakeville takes property by Eminent Domain - Partners divided money equally after 16 years back taxes were paid

- All Cassidy's settle in Winter Haven FL and become wealthy owning their own real estate businesses.

- The Warburtons retired to Winter Haven. Ethel died and was buried there in 1988.

Note: Ted became part of the Cassidy family and visited often while coaching hitting to Red Sox
players in training in Winter Haven, FL. Albert B. Cassidy - son of Albert H. (Founder of Camp) became close to Ted and knew many of Teds close friends. Ted asked him to be Executor of his estate when he died. Albert B. accepted the job.

Note: Cassidys and Warburtons all ended up living in Winter Haven, FL after the Boys Baseball Camp closed in 1986. Ethel died and was buried there in 1988. Lester died in 1998 and they are now buried in the Sampson Cemetery, Bedford St., Lakeville. The land occupied by the Cemetery was donated by the Boston Council of Boy Scouts to a private party in 1944, before the Scout property was purchased by Ted Williams in 1957 and it became the Boys Baseball Camp.

It is fitting that they are resting on the property they worked so hard to preserve

Note: 1948 was the beginning of the Jimmy fund. Ted participated then and for the rest of his life, giving of his time to visit children being treated for cancer. The boy Jimmy was in reality Einar Gustuf son a 12-year-old who became the symbol of the fund. Ted (age 81) - met Einar (age 63) for the first time in Boston.

Ted visited children sick with cancer without any public notice through-out his legacy years in Lakeville (1957 - 1986) Joe LoRusso, a Ted Williams Camper, coach and counselor from 1975- 1986 began a Ted Williams semi-annual Alumnai and Jimmy Fund benefit at the Camp in Lakeville in 1993 which continues today and into the future. Lester Warburtons daughter Joanne, and Albert H. Cassidy's daughter Carol, were Girls Day Campers, and have attended the benefits.

ABOUT THE AUTHOR

Ed Leonard is a graduate mechanical engineer with a career in sales and management for the Foxboro Co., a manufacturer of industrial control equipment and process control systems in Foxboro, MA. Ed has traveled extensively across the USA, visiting all 50 states plus all the Canadian border provinces, developing an interest in history, and producing documentation of his family history dating back to the 1600s. He wrote a description of the development of the golf ball with examples now on display at the Easton Country Club in Easton, MA., and he documented a single-page description of 1800 Civil War Monuments existing in the USA, which resides with the Civil War History Museum in Vernon, CT. Ed has enjoyed the sports of tennis and golf but never participated in baseball, fishing, or hunting. He is a product of the Depression era and was aware at 8 of the popular Red Sox and Ted Williams while listening to games on the radio on a warm summer afternoon.

The Ted Williams Boys Baseball Camp was established in 1957 in the small town of Lakeville, MA and is where Ed has lived in retirement for the past 18 years. The recently released book, "THE WINGMEN," drew Ed's attention to an innocuous statement: "Ted made occasional cameo appearances at the annual Ted Williams Camp in Lakeville, MA."

This is a misleading statement. Ted lived in Lakeville every summer for 8 years from 1961 - 1968, supervising the operation of his Boys Baseball Camp with three local regular guys as partners. In 1969, he left Lakeville to become the manager of the Washington Senators and returned for two or three weeks every year to continue supervision until 1986, when the Camp closed. Under his direction, the Camp assisted young boys and girls to become disciplined adults while enjoying the game of baseball and other athletic activities and forming long-lasting friendships.

The full story exceeded expectations, defining a "Legacy that has been overlooked" until now with this book. It follows Ted's first legacy as "The greatest hitter who ever lived," followed by his second legacy, serving his country as a decorated military fighter pilot. His Legacy continues today in Lakeville with a day of activities attended by former Ted Williams Campers Alumni and Friends raising money for The Jimmy fund, which annually raises money for the continuation of cancer research by the Dana Farber Cancer Institute, a charity that Ted actively participated in beginning in the 1940s.

Made in the USA
Las Vegas, NV
12 March 2025

ace35d3c-03fd-4e28-947f-55dd61c25bc9R01